BURIED IN THE DARK

Joy Ifeyinwa Ubani

Unless otherwise indicated, all Scripture quotations are taken from the *New King James Version* of the Bible.

Book Express Publishing House books may be ordered through booksellers or www.goexpresspublishing.com.

ISBN: 978-1-955495-06-6 (Paperback)
ISBN 978-1-955495-07-3 (Hardback)
ISBN: 978-1-955495-08-0 (ebook)

Printed in the United States of America
Print information available on the last page.
Library of Congress Control Number: 2021939096 (Paperback)

BOOK EXPRESS PUBLISHING HOUSE
Atlanta, Georgia
www.goexpressbulishing.com

CONTENT

PROLOGUE

And we know that all things work together for good to them that love God, to those who are called according to His purpose. For whom He did foreknew, He also did predestined to be conformed to the image of His Son, that he might be the firstborn amongst many brethren.

— Romans 8:28-29

For too many women and children, home is far from being safe. Yearly, hundreds of millions of women and children are exposed to domestic violence at homes, communities, organizations, schools, workplaces, etc. This has a powerful and adverse effect on their lives and hopes for the future. A ten-year-old child that lives in a violent home in the United Kingdom says, "My sister and I are so scared, our parents always fight, and we fear they might break up."

Gender-based violence knows no borders, knows no socio-economic sector, knows no educational sector, and knows no color. It is part of our society; we cannot pinpoint one part of the community that is more exposed to it because it crosses all boundaries. Globally, statistics suggest that one in five women have been exposed to physical abuse. In the U.S., approximately three women are killed every day by a current or former intimate partner. In South Africa, a woman is killed every four hours. In some countries like Pakistan or some parts of African countries, many men believe that they are entitled to use violence against their partners and their children to compel compliance with whatever the man wants. The brutal irony is that should a victim speak up about physical, sexual, or emotional abuse, she would be seen as having lost her family dignity. Many rapes go unreported and unpunished as most victims are afraid that they will become worthless in society.

This book of thirteen Chapters brings out inspiration to the downtrodden, gives hope to the hopeless, encouragement, and strength to those suffering from one form of abuse or the other, both young and old, man or woman, boy or girl. Keep hope and faith alive. It can be difficult to see beyond what is currently happening in your life and see the light at the end of the tunnel in tough and uncertain times. Whether you are going through a big life challenge, a hard time for your family, or a personal health concern, an optimistic frame of mind can help you see a difficult challenge as an opportunity for gratitude. When you are feeling low, try to find the silver linings in your hardship. "For I know the plans I have for you declares the Lord, plans to prosper you and not to harm you, plans to give you hope and a future" (Jeremiah 29:11). There is undoubtedly a future for you, and your hope will not be cut off. Always trust God, be resilient, persevere, be patient, work hard, be strong, have faith, and be focused. Everything will be all right in His time.

— Dr. Joy Ifeyinwa Ubani

ABOUT THE BOOK

Born into a poverty-stricken household, fate threw the young Chizoba into a path she wouldn't have considered treading if given an option. And the more she fought to escape the clutches of poverty, the more she found herself sinking deeper into it. It was as if misfortunes were trailing her every step. The unrelenting embers of a tumultuous society complicated her life's journey that no matter how hard she fought to live a normal life, things kept spiraling out of control.

Will she be swallowed by calamities or salvaged by destiny? A mystery soon to be unraveled.

BURIED IN THE DARK

CHAPTER ONE

"The spirits still seem to have an overload of work," Dike subconsciously mumbled. The darkness of the night from his thatch-roofed hut was still immeasurably thick and impenetrable that seeing his hand was a distant possibility. He had applied all the art and science of time determination in his ambiance yet to no avail. Maybe the spirits are having a busy time in the world of the living and had decided to confuse man's knowledge of nature by seizing the day on its way, he thought to himself. It is a held belief that the dead roam the night while the living sleeps and that one might encounter them if he goes out in the night. Whether his or her spirit will be taken along to the land of the dead depends on the kind of spirit encountered, either benevolent or malevolent. It seemed the cock too was a shareholder in this state of confusion because even the early morning crow had not been heard. The little fire under his bamboo bed had long gone out.

Tired of laying down, Dike rose to his feet. He staggered and reached out for his "manjara" - a local lantern constructed by making a small hole on the cork of an empty multi-vite bottle and forcing a thread through it, powered by either kerosene or paraffin. He lighted the lantern, undid the bent nail which served as the internal lock of his window, and peered vacuously into the dark void. Nothing of this nature had happened before to the best of his knowledge. Or does it mean he woke up earlier than usual, he wondered. He opened his door, and with the lantern in his hand, set out to his wife's hut to be sure all was well.

The compound embodies four huts enclosed with dwarf bamboo fences—one at the front center and the others in opposite directions. The center hut house was built for Dike, while the other three were built for his three wives and children. Also adjacent to the building is his "obi," and at the back of the huts is his barn, where he keeps his farm produce and hunting equipment.

At the window of the second wife's hut, Dike quietened himself and listened. The snore vibrating from within the hut suggests that of a sound sleep with sweet dreams, though he can't ascertain whether it was that of his wife or her mother, he is so convinced they are fine. His second wife had given birth two days back, and her mother had come for "omugwo" as tradition demands. 'Omugwo' is an Igbo word used to describe the practice in which a nursing mother and her baby are taken care of by a close family member. In most cases, it is done by the mother or mother-in-law except in the case where they are not available, then another immediate female family member steps in. This practice usually lasts from three to five months from the date of the child's birth.

A male child he would have preferred, but the gift of children belongs to the Almighty God, and who dares question him? At least he is happy the woman had finally succeeded in given him a fruit after consecutively having five miscarriages. According to the local doctor, she wouldn't be able to give birth again after suffering from many complications during childbirth. "Thank goodness I even have one now," he said, "I pray her fate becomes different."

In some tribes in Africa, the preference for a male child is very prevalent and exists in several cultures as it dates to prehistoric times, and it is tied to inheritance. Unfortunately, it has not succumbed to societal changes but has remained sacrosanct because of the desire for a male child to carry on the family name and guarantee the family lineage. Because of this preference, there is usually immense pressure on wives to give birth to male children. In addition to placing women in a situation in which they inadvertently encourage women's inferior position through the preference for male children, this directly affects them in making reproductive decisions and affects their psyche. The Igbos are an ethnic group in the South-Eastern part of Nigeria with a strong penchant for patriarchy. Women who give birth to a child who is a girl in Igbo land are unhappy at their first delivery because of the fear of rejection and disappointment from their husbands. A man is viewed from the angle of male children he can owe claims to, and it goes a long way to determine the size of his farm during the farming seasons. This can explain the dominance of polygamy among many Igbo families. One is held in high esteem considering the number of male children he has.

Something has moved in the second hut. What could that be, he feared. The memories emanating from the first wife's hut can make even the strongest helpless. Who is there? He rattled. No sound could be heard again. Being a hunter, at least he is fearless to some extent. He carefully trod into the hut and couldn't find anyone or see anything. Maybe the spirit of Obiageli and her children still play hide and seek there, or probably it might be a rat. But a rat doesn't make such sound, he reasoned. Whatever that could be, what one does not know should not be the source of his death. With fear cooking up in him, he hurried back to his hut. It was still very dark into the unfathomable dead of the night. The noise he heard from his first wife's hut still sounds in his thoughts. He sat on his agada - a locally made collapsible wooden chair. The gods have not really been fair to me, he said, lost in thought.

Anyone who knew Dike very well would undoubtedly think that an unknown spirit cursed him. The possibility of him having killed a spirit in an animal form is the opinion held by many. Because of the wealth his father left behind, this is a man who should have been among the rich men of Amaokwu village or certainly the richest, but life has indeed not been fair. Not long after his father died, his mother was stricken by an unknown sickness that defied all medications. Dike had to auction out almost all his lands to save the life of a jewel he cherished most. Stories had it that being the last in his family, Dike was so much endeared to the mother that he never stopped being breastfed until he was eleven. No wonder he had to give in so much to salvage the life of the love of his life, but the saying that money can elongate but can't buy life gives credence to her death. Only if he had known she wouldn't survive the ailment more could have been saved? The misfortune that had befallen him some years back is what any sane man would never wish his fellow. As if losing both parents the same year wasn't enough, his first wife and her six children followed suit.

Dike had gone to Amauwani, his maternal home, to attend a traditional marriage ceremony, only to be greeted with the heartbreaking news of the death of his eldest wife and her children on his arrival the next day. On a fateful day, Obiageli had made her favorite food of "ukwa," which she and her children ate. As is the customary family rite of eating from one pot, Adanma also partook in the meal, which would best be regarded as the last supper following a later incident. Bidding each other the usual night wish after the dinner, both wives retired to their hut for the night cause. Mixed feelings arose when no sign of life was heard from Obiageli's hut the following day. On reaching the hut, Adanma observed that the door was securely locked from the outside, but the most surprising of it all was that such was unprecedented. She had never left that early and even without throwing her greetings. Even the fact that she left with all her children fueled the aired suspicion. All was thought to be well, not until flies were seen hovering around the hut later that day and with a perceived foul smell. Adanma alerted some neighbors who helped her break the door, only to be opened to an obscene scene. There lay helplessly the lifeless body of Obiageli and her six children. Only if wailing could change anything, Adanma would have been a heroic savior. She would have joined them if not for the appropriate intervention of the neighbors.

The tears she shed that day alone were quite enough to irrigate a farm in the dry season. The worst is that she became the prime suspect being the only one at home. She was only exonerated to innocence after swearing at the great Odukwu shrine and remained alive afterward. The great Odukwu shrine is highly dreaded and powerful that any false swear made at its feet warrants immediate death by the striking of thunder. The person who locked the door to their hut, Adanma being alive after eating the same food and swearing, and the real cause of their death remains a mystery. Even the gods have decided to be calm on the issue.

Osinachi, the third wife, was killed on her way back from their village stream. The death, too, had occurred years back, even before Obiageli and her children's demise. It was during the dry season, and the humidity was hostile in the evening of that fateful day. Osinachi, in her traditional costume, had gone to take her bath in Osukwu stream, where she was raped to death by a group of unknown men. The crow of the cock brought Dike back to the realm of consciousness. He looked through the window. He had been so engrossed in thought that he failed to notice when the slow and heavy wheels of dawn finally brought it home. By now, the morning had become old and full-blown as to permit far-away sight.

Dike quickly stood up from his agada. This early morning, he had to go to the forest to check whether his trap had laid hold of an animal. He hurriedly made for his inner room, brought out kola nut, his snuff-box, and a bottle of aromatic schnapps, and in a procession-like manner proceeded to his little shrine near his" obi" to perform his morning ritual. After breaking kola nut and pouring libations to his "Chi" and ancestors in prayer for success, he went and sat in his "Obi" to take some snuffs. Snuff had become a part of him, that staying a day without taking it might fast-forward his death. Even the local doctor had told him to give it a quit, but that's the last thing Dike of all people would do. According to him, being dead is better than quitting what makes you happy because that is the essence of living." He brought out his snuff-box, hit it three consecutive times with his thumb, screwed it open, and began to feed his nostrils with that dark-brown powdery substance.

At the end of this arduous task, he went back to his hut to get his hunting equipment. Fully prepared to leave, he went straight to his wife's hut, greeted them, kissed the baby girl, and set out to the forest. That was the last anyone saw or heard of him again. Whether he had been killed by an animal or an enemy or still alive is what no one could ascertain. A search party was organized in search of him both within and outside Amaokwu village. Not even a sign of his belonging was seen. The primary truth is that Dike is no more, leaving the family behind with absolutely nothing.

After two weeks, her husband had gone missing, and her mother - Uloaku, died, leaving only her and the young Chizoba in this cruel world. Life became very unbearable and each day filled with difficulties and trials. Notwithstanding the cruelty of life to her, Adanma remained a virtuous woman who had a strong value attached to womanhood and the likes. She distinguished herself from those promiscuous and sluttish women in the village. A lot happened as her husband's kinsmen and friends tried taking advantage of her condition. Being a poor widow left with nothing but her only child, it was very hard for her. From the perspective of those men who gallivant and jazz around looking for any available hole to swim into, Adanma would be a good and easy catch. Still, to their uttermost chagrin and bewilderment, she always proved them wrong as she would firmly and intensively place a decline to all their filthy and nasty requests to make out with her. She never cared about the offers made to her as long as her prime, worth, and self-reputation were at stake. This brought about hatred amongst her and these promiscuous men, but she never regarded this as one of her predicaments.

Days turned into nights, weeks flew into months, and years kept moving. Adanma and her daughter Chizoba were living fine. Though they were suffering, the tranquility of life was still theirs to possess. Adaptability to the new life was their only option. The little Chizoba had grown to be a young girl with a well-domesticated character and morals inculcated in her by her mother. She was intelligent, hardworking, and respectful. Chizoba would always encourage her mom as little as she was whenever she got the insight and instinct that her mother was becoming weak and fainting due to the hardship. Adanma and her daughter "Chizoba" had a parcel of been merciful to us; at least we can still afford daily food and, as such, are content with the little we have. With all due respect, my daughter can't be allowed to be somebody's second wife talk more of the seventh." She said. She also made him understand that her daughter is still very tender for marriage, so he is on an impossible mission. Dikeukwu persuaded her and offered a lot of wealth to her and promised to take care of her and her daughter, but she bluntly declined without prevarication.

He has always been a man who gets whatsoever he wanted and had never faced such humiliation before in his life, and now the insult is coming from one whom he considers a wretch. Amidst anger and aggravation, with a feeling of disgruntlement about how the poor woman was able to choose pride instead of his benevolence, he was raged, and he left furiously. Rumors they say fly more than an airplane. The story of what transpired between Ichie Dikeukwu and Adanma went viral in the village that they became the talk of the moment. Adanma couldn't afford to let go of her child into early marriage. She believes it's a form of slavery because she was still little and was not ready to compromise due to the hardship she was passing through with her young daughter.

"Mother, who was the man that came earlier?" Chizoba asked.

"It was nothing serious, my daughter; it was just a casual visit," her mother quickly replied to avoid further questions.

Chizoba has indeed been helpful and a great sort of comfort to Adanma. She does help with anything she could be of help. She would fetch water and firewood for her even without being asked to. She derives joy whenever she is helping her mother out. No doubt, the only thing still keeping Adanma and energizing her to live on is the joy she derives whenever she looks at her daughter, who never relents in being the good girl she has always wished for her. She would look at her daughter, and with excitement and delight, thank God for such a gift to her. Chizoba was indeed a good company to her.

Ichie Dikeukwu couldn't still fathom what could have given Adanma such audacity to turn down his offer. To placate his anger, he reached a resolution to deal with Adanma and her daughter in the most iniquitous manner. The following morning, Adanma and her daughter had gone to their farm to make some harvests. The next day would be Eke market, and they needed some cash

CHAPTER TWO

That was exactly ten years back. The little Chizoba had now moved to stay with her aunt in the City. Due to the hard nature of life they were experiencing and for an enabling purpose of responsibility, Adanma had sought help from her immediate younger sister, who lives in the City. Nneka and her husband have been bonded by marriage for the past decade and five years with no recorded issue (child), not even a miscarriage. However, her husband seemed not to be much disturbed by this development, understanding fully well that child-bearing is a gift from God and not necessarily her doing.

Mama Uka (Ukadike's mother) had waited for such a long time to hear the good news of childbirth or even pregnancy from Ukadike and his wife, yet none was forthcoming. She decided to visit her son the following weekend to ascertain the cause of their problem. She went over to the call center in their village to phone his son and tell him of her intending visit.

Mama Uka: “How are you and your wife Nna m?”

“Hope all is well, my son,” she asked.

Ukadike: “Yes, mama, we are fine, and you?”

Mama Uka: “I’m fine too, just some little sicknesses associated with old age, but notwithstanding, I’m fine, my son.”

“Good to hear,” Ukadike retorted.

Mama Uka: “I called to notify you that I would be coming over by the weekend, and I would need some money for transportation,” she told her son.

Ukadike: “No problem, mama, I will send the money across to you,” Ukadike told her.

Ukadike was delighted to hear that his mother intends to visit. It was indeed a welcomed development. He couldn’t wait to have a taste of “okpa,” his favorite, which his mother always brings anytime she’s coming. The mother is such a good cook that having a taste of her food can make one come for her daughter's hand in marriage to have a leeway passage for more. Stories have it that her first daughter's husband had come to visit one of his friends in the village, and the friend had taken him to Mama Ukadike's restaurant. On eating the food, he never had rest of mind any longer until he tied the knot with her daughter due to the delicious nature of the meal he had. Just like the Oliver Twist tendency, any man that feeds from the pot of Mama Ukadike would definitely come seeking more.

"No problem, mama, I will send the money across to you," Ukadike told his mom, and the call ended. Ukadike told his wife the news about his mom's visitation, and the look on his wife's face was a sign of bewilderment. Her woman instinct already told her the ulterior reason behind the visitation. She was not happy about the oncoming visitation.

Mama arrived so early on Friday morning; she had taken a night bus to the City. When their doorbell rang, Nneka was so surprised seeing Mama at the door; though they anticipated her visitation but never expected it to be this early in the morning. Mama Uka had left in the night to the City to avoid traffic. The traffic congestion is something that usually bores her about the City. They reached around three in the morning, and she slept at the park, waiting for the darkness to give way. Immediately it was dawn; she left the park for her son's house.

"You are welcome, Mama, "Nneka greeted her mother-in-law with a hug.

"Thank you, my daughter, "she had replied.

After a warm welcome and familiar pleasantry, Mama was served the delicacy prepared ahead because of her coming. The way she licked her fingers while eating the "egusi soup" and her fastness in voraciously devouring the heaped pounded yam was a clear indication that she enjoyed every bit of the meal. Later in the day, after dinner, they discussed family issues and crises in the village before they retired for the day. In the morning of the next day, Mama Uka called on his son to unknot and reveal to him her main ulterior reason for coming.

"My son, you are not getting any younger, and at this stage of your life, all you need is a baby, a boy who would take over your business in case of any misfortune. This is the twelfth year of your married life with no issue yet. I am your mother, and you can always count on me, so feel free to tell me whose fault it is amongst both of you, then we can look for the best possible way to solve the problem. I need to carry my grandchild," Mama Uka said to her son. Ukadike was shocked to hear this. He was perplexed because he never perceived this could be the reason his mother had called to visit. "Mama, please, I'm in no haste or desperate of having a child. Only God gives children, and they are a gift from him. I believe at God's own appointed time he would bless us with our own children," Ukadike replied, ending the discussion halfway.

Back in the village, some rumor mongers had already spread that Nneka in her youth indulged in countless abortions before she got married to Ukadike, which was the reason for her purported barrenness. Considering the love Ukadike had for his wife, he would always give deaf ears to such rumors. Mama Uka was displeased by how her son had reacted to her good intent about his success, so she decided to do it her way. She suddenly changed over Nneka. She would constantly ask her the reason behind her barrenness which she would have no answer to. This question would always make Nneka break down into tears, but those tears were seen as fake and were referred to as "crocodile tears" by her mother-in-law.

On several occasions, Mama Uka insulted the hell out of Nneka and demanded her to urge her husband to take in another wife since she was unable to give him a child. Or better still, divorce her son. Seeing that her actions were not yielding any success, she would constantly call her names whenever her husband had left for work. "You wretched and barren witch; could it be that the human sympathy in you is dead or what? Why on earth would you choose to captivate and shackle my son into your barrenness; why can't you just let him go and carry your bad fate alone?" Mama Uka mocked her.

This was really becoming unbearable for Nneka; she would cry and cry until there would be no tears left to cry. She would always relate to her husband the whole insult and mockery made to her by his mother. Ukadike always got infuriated after hearing these complaints about his mom and had warned her seriously. He threatened to send her back to the village if she continued. The loads of abuse she does get from her mother-in-law is so much and can sure make one consider choosing suicide as an option. That very weekend was indeed a sad one for her.

Her husband's house always turns into something else for her anytime her mother-in-law is around. She even had to bring along with her another woman for his son to marry during one of her visits. Several times Nneka had been called a witch and a barren by her mother-in-law. As a measure to curb this and ensure peace and stability in his home, Ukadike had restricted his mother from coming to his house uninvited while providing her with everything she needed in the village.

Ukadike and his wife have sown seed in every known church and ministries in town, yet all efforts seemed like pouring water on a stone. She had prayed on several occasions to be blessed with a child, even if a cripple. Pregnancy was very far from sight. She once went to the hospital thinking she was pregnant only to be told that she overfed and no baby was in her stomach. Though laughable, it may seem, but it only added much agony to her woes. They keep trusting God to bless them one day with a child of their own, being confident that they both are okay health-wise.

During one of their visits to Adanma in the village and seeing her pitiful condition cum the hardship that had befallen her and for the fact that they had no child of their own, they agreed to take Chizoba with them to the City. Chizoba's joy knew no bounds the very day she left for the City. She had heard so many enticing stories about the City from her friends in their village school. As it had become their custom, during the first week at the expiration of every term holiday, they do gather around the mango tree at the center of their school during each break period. This is usually the time when those that are privileged to have traveled to the city unleash the tiger in their tongues, making others feel less human. This set of people are called the celebrities, and the kind of respect accorded them by their village contemporaries is unexplainable.

She had heard of so many White-Wonders present in the City. One of the celebrities had it that the City's gutters were all decorated with bulbs and that the lights direct the flow of rushing water in the gutter. Being a young girl, she already had a big dream to make her poor mother proud and get liberated and emancipated from the shackles of poverty. She had heard stories of celebrities and influential people in society, and she really felt going to the City would be a great opportunity on her side. Chizoba's dream has always been to go and behold the City, even if for thirty seconds. She really wanted to see the possibility of how people do enter the small bird that usually flies high past their village house. She couldn't wait to be a celebrity to be accorded due respect. Only if she knew she wouldn't be coming back anytime soon.

Her mother had told her that she would be going for a vacation to the City at the end of the term. The radiant beam of smile that filled her face is a clear picture of one that is soon to accomplish a long-term goal. To cut a long story short, she started preparing bit by bit from that day. Only if she knew she was not going to see her mother again for so long a time. Being her only parent, she grew up to know, she had been so entangled to her and would have even rejected the City's offer just to be with her. She understands her plight very well and never did or planned to do anything that would break her heart.

Life in the City is different from that of the village. So many eye-catching things caught her gaze. A mere look at her reveals that she is a "journey just come" - a slang used to describe a novice in the City. Even her mode of dressing is an excellent pointer to that fact. She has finally been exposed to the wonders she's been hearing about and can't wait to go back to the village to receive her own crown of respect.

The family gave Chizoba a warm welcome. Since they had no child of their own, she became the apple of their eye. They seemed not to allow her to do anything that might prove difficult. If only my mom were here to enjoy all this with me, she said. She had long started missing her mother and some of her school friends though the good life she enjoys here made this less intense. She was finally made to understand that she was already in her new home and should dust the home-sick act out of her memory. This was indeed a big blow for her, but she considered the fact that she could do nothing. Also, for the sake that she'd been shown a great deal of love, she now chose adaptability.

CHAPTER THREE

The hope of the righteous is gladness, but the expectation of the wicked perishes.

— Proverb 10:28

Before Chizoba arrived at Nneka's house in the City, Nneka decided to foster a little child of about eight years because of her inability to have a child of her own. It was a wet and stormy day in April. Downpour pounded on the windows as she arranged for Ugomma's (Nneka's child of about eight years) coming. She was expected in the early afternoon; however, Nneka was sure she'd be early. Nneka remained in what was to be Ugomma's new room and attempted to see it through a child's eyes.

"Was it engaging and inviting?" She had adorned its walls with brilliantly shaded banners of creatures and purchased another comforter with a giant print of a teddy bear on it. She also positioned a couple of delicate toys on the bed, even though she was certain that Ugomma, having lived with her parents, uncles, and aunts, would probably have a few belongings.

The room looked cheerful and energetic than an eight-year-old young girl might want as her bedroom. All it required was its new occupant. Nneka looked around; at that point, she came out and shut the entryway, fulfilled she had done a great beautification. Proceeding with the arrival, she closed all the room doors. When it came to showing Ugomma around, it was essential to guarantee she got privacy and confidentiality. This would be simpler if the standard rules were built up directly from the beginning.

Downstairs, she busied herself in the kitchen. It's going to be a hasty day, and even after such a long time of staying alone, she was a little anxious. Another kid's arrival is a significant occasion for her family, maybe as much with respect to the kid herself. She trusted Ukadike would show up sooner than expected so that both of them would have a quiet chat and offer moral help before the huge arrival.

Not long before noon early afternoon, the doorbell rang. She made way for the door to find Muna, drenching wet from his walk from the bus station. Muna is an apprentice living with them for a few years and has been of enormous help to them in getting things done. She guided him in, offered him a coffee, and left him cleaning his forehead in the lounge while she came back to the kitchen. Before the pot could heat up, the bell rang once more. She went to the entryway, hoping to see Ukadike on the doorstep, hitherto it was the link worker from yesterday, Udoka, alongside another lady, who was grinning fearlessly.

"This is Chioma, my colleague,' said Udoka, dispensing with small talk. 'And, this is Ugomma (the little girl)." Nneka looked down; however, Ugomma was holding up behind Chioma, and everything she could see was a couple of strong legs in splendid red pants.

"Hello dear, Ugomma,' Nneka said dazzlingly. I'm Nneka. It's ideal to meet you. Come on in." Ugomma was sticking to Chioma's jacket and decided she wasn't going anywhere, as Chioma out of nowhere pulled in reverse, almost losing her balance. 'Try not to be senseless,' snapped Udoka, who made a grab behind her colleague. Ugomma was faster and more grounded, for Chioma took another reel, this time sideways. Fortunately, their old cat decided to place in a well-timed appearance, walking languidly down the lobby. She took her signal. 'Look who's come to see you, Ugomma!' she cried, the energy in her voice messed up with regards to our fat and torpid muggy. 'It's Tochia (their cat). She's come to say hello!'

Ugomma peeped from Chioma's waist to see the cat. Ugomma had dark hair set in ponytails. It was evident that her previous keepers had been so careless in taking care of her from her look. Under her clothes, she was wearing a yellow shirt, blue singlet, and wellies. No reasonable adult would have dressed a child that way. Unmistakably, Ugomma was accustomed to having her own specific manner. With her interest incited, she chose to take a closer look at the cat and gave Chioma another push, sending them both faltering over the doorstep and into the corridor. Udoka followed, and the cat reasonably nipped out. Nneka immediately shut the door. 'It's gone!' Ugomma hollered, her face squeezed with outrage. 'Don't worry; she'll be back soon. We should get you out of your wet coat.' Before the cat's loss could grow into a scene, she fixed her zip and attempted to redirect her attention. 'Muna's in the garden waiting for you.'

She gazed for a second but mentioning Muna's name; a recognizable name attracted her attention. She removed her coat and stepped intensely down to the garden to meet Muna. 'I need that cat,' she snarled at Muna. Chioma and Udoka looked at each other surprisingly, which could be interpreted as 'God have Mercy on this lady.' Nneka offered them coffee while they walked together to the garden. Ugomma saw a box of building blocks and sat comfortably on the ground, crossed-legged on the floor, making some efforts to fix the building block box together.

Nneka went back to the kitchen, brought out a few cups, and began to pour coffee on each. She heard a loud noise in the doorway then Ugomma showed up. She looked so odd, not charming, or beautiful; however, Nneka assumed that was because of the aggressive way she held her face and body, like persistently careful.

'What's in here?' Ugomma questioned her, pulling the kitchen cabinet open.

'Cutlery,' Nneka said unnecessarily, as the subsequent clack had reported itself.

'What?' she demanded, scowling at her. 'Cutlery?'

Nneka replied, 'It's knives, forks, and spoons. We'll eat with it later during dinner, and you need to tell me what you like to eat.'

Ugomma left the cabinet and moved to the next and the subsequent, opening the mall. At first, Nneka wasn't worried about her curiosity; that was normal. What baffled her more was the rage and furiousness in the entirety of Ugomma's movement, which she had never observed so pronounced before. Ugomma opened all the drawers in the kitchen, and the kettle bubbled. She took out a plate and a biscuit and requested to have them, lurching for the packet. Nneka gently stopped her and asked her to close the drawers; else, they will thud upon them.

She took a closer look at her with a problematic and insubordinate gaze. Had anyone prevented her from doing anything, or was she purposely trying her? There was a couple of moments of interruption, a standstill, while she thought of her request. Nneka saw how overweight she was. From Ugomma's overweight, it was evident that she'd been comfortable eating or had been offered food to keep her calm, most likely both. 'Please,' 'Please,' she said reassuringly and began to close the drawers. She watched, at that point, with two hands pummeled the closest cabinet energetically.

'Delicately, like this.' Nneka illustrated.

However, Nneka didn't offer any more help and didn't compel the issue because Ugomma just barely arrived and had at least made an attempt by shutting one.

Ugomma demanded to have the biscuits again, this time more loudly. 'I'd like your assistance. I'm certain you're good at helping, right? Said Nneka.'

'Ugomma, please take this into the garden and offer everyone a biscuit, then take one for yourself, good?'

Nneka put the plate in Ugomma's hand, hoping that she would deliver the biscuit safely at the garden, then followed her with the tray of beverages, satisfied that she'd done as she'd desired. She handed out the cups of coffee as the doorbell rang, flagging their last arrival. Ugomma jumped up and made a scramble for the door. Nneka immediately followed; it's bad practice for a young girl to be answering the door, regardless of whether visitors are expected. She disclosed this to Ugomma, at which point they opened the door together. Ukadike stood on the doorstep. He was grinning calmingly and looked down at the dreary confronted child gazing rebelliously up at him.

'Hi,' said Ukadike splendidly. 'You should be Ugomma.'

'I needed to do it,' fought Ugomma before stepping down the lobby to re-join the others.

'Is everything okay?' Ukadike asked as he came in.

'Alright, so far. No serious catastrophes yet, anyway,' Nneka replied.

Nneka took Ukadike's jacket, and he went through to the lounge and got another coffee for him while they started the desk work. Basically, when a kid is placed with a new guardian, they are required to fill in some forms. Muna was writing irately.

He had just barely finished the last movie, he said happily. "Is it Nneka with an N?' She affirmed that it was, at that moment, given him her home address and her doctor's name and address. Ugomma, who'd been sensibly content watching him, and had been involved with the procedure many times previously, concluded it was time to walk around once more. She pulled herself up and vanished into the kitchen. Nneka couldn't permit her to be in there alone; very aware of the danger of her raiding the cupboards, many implements could be unsafe in inappropriate hands. She called her, yet she didn't respond. She walked in and discovered her attempting to yank open the cupboard under the sink, which was ensured by a child lock, as it contained the different cleaning items.

'Please, Ugomma, leave that for the time being. Let's go into the garden,' she said. 'I'll show you around later. We'll make out time once they've gone.' 'I need a drink,' Ugomma requested, pulling more diligently on the cupboard door. 'Alright, but it's not in there.' She opened the right cabinet, where Nneka kept a range of squashes. She looked in at the line of brilliantly hued bottles. 'Orange, lemon, blackcurrant, or apple?' Nneka offered. 'Coke,' she demanded.

'I'm sorry, there's no Coke. It's awful for your teeth.' 'What about apples? Tina, my god-daughter, likes apples. You'll meet her later.' 'That one.'

She attempted to get onto the work surface to recover the bottle. She brought down the blackcurrant bottle, poured the drink, then helped it through and set it on the table. Nneka drew up the kid measuring wicker seat, which is typically a most loved, and told Ugomma it's the correct size for her, 'her very own seat.' Ugomma disregarded her, grabbed her glass, and plopped herself in the spot where Nneka sat on the couch close to Ukadike and close to Muna, while Ukadike appeased Ugomma with a game on his cell phone. Nneka watched her for a couple of seconds.

So, this is the kid who is going to be living with us. It was difficult to make much about her at an early stage; most kids show troublesome behavior in their initial few days in another home. Nonetheless, there was an uncommon attitude about her that she couldn't precisely comprehend: it was anger, obviously, and willfulness, blended in with something different that she didn't know she had seen previously. Just time would tell. Nneka watched Ugomma's awkward movements and the way her tongue lolled over her base lip. She noted culpably how it gave her a dull, empty air and advised herself that she was categorized as having just 'mild' learning challenges instead of 'severe.' A quarter of an hour later, all the placement forms had been finished. Nneka endorsed them, and Muna gave her duplicates. Udoka and Chioma instantly stood to leave.

Nneka immediately put on her shoes and coat, and they got steadily doused as they went back and forth to the vehicle; then, the two ladies said a brisk farewell to Ugomma. She ignored them, clearly feeling the rejection. Muna remained for an additional ten minutes, chatting with Ugomma about Nneka and their home, then he, too, made a move to leave.

Ugomma smiled, steering up to Muna, 'I want to come,' she smiled, 'Take me with you. I want to go in your car.'

'I don't have a car,' said Muna quietly. 'Also, you're staying with Nneka. Remember we discussed it? This is your dazzling new home now.'

As Muna picked his briefcase and got halfway to the doorway, Ugomma opened her mouth wide and shouted. It was ear-piercing. Nneka surged over and put her arms around her, and gestured to Muna to go. He sneaked out, and she held her until the noise died down. There were no tears, yet her previously pale cheeks were now flushed bright red. The last individual left was Ukadike.

'Will you be good, Nneka?' he asked as he prepared to move into the downpour. 'I'll telephone around four.' He realized that the sooner Ugomma and Nneka were left alone, the sooner she'd settle.

'We'll be fine, won't we, Ugomma?' Nneka said. 'I'll show you around, and afterward, we'll unpack.'

She had compassion for the poor girl and her odd behavior. Nneka held her hands as they saw Ukadike off, remaining only both of them. Nneka has had this type of experience before, welcoming a befuddled and hurt little girl into her home, standing persistently as they got accustomed to one another and an unusual environment. However, this felt distinctive somehow. There was something unusual in Ugomma's eyes that were chilling. She hadn't seen it previously in a child or a grown-up. She reminded herself that Ugomma was just a little girl, and she had twenty years of experience in caring for children.

Nneka led her back into the living room, and Tochia reappeared. She showed Ugomma the right way to stroke her. However, she lost enthusiasm when she started. 'I'm hungry. I want a biscuit.' Ugomma made a splash for the kitchen. Nneka followed behind her to clarify that too many biscuits aren't acceptable when she noticed a pungent smell. 'Ugomma, do you want to use the toilet?' she asked calmly. She shook her head. 'Would you like to poop?' 'No!' She smiled, and before she understood what she was doing, her hand was in her jeans, and she spread feces over her face.

'Ugomma!' she seized her wrist, frightened.

She groveled instantly, protecting her face. 'You going to hit me?' 'No, Ugomma. Obviously not. I'd never do that. You will have a shower, and next time inform me when you need the toilet. You're a big girl now.' Slowly, Nneka led her upstairs, and she followed, awkward, ambling and her face spread with feces. What had she let herself into, said Nneka?

CHAPTER FOUR

Nneka asked Ugomma not to thump, kick, bite or push Kate, Tina, her, or anybody. 'It harms; it's terrible. Do you understand?' She said nothing. Kate and Tina are god-daughters of Nneka who came for a short visit at Nneka's house. It was almost 2 pm on Saturday, the day after Ugomma had arrived, and the girls had come down the stairs after their weekend lie-in. Ugomma welcomed Kate with a kick. 'I would prefer not to tell you once more, said Nneka to Ugomma. Do I make myself clear?' She pulled a face and stepped off a few doors down. 'Apologies, Kate,' Nneka said. Kate shrugged. We knew there was very little to be done about Ugomma's horrendous attitude but to continue reinforcing that it was terrible and that she mustn't do it. A moment later, Ugomma reappeared, her fist clenched and excoriating the air. She started behaving abnormally and shouting, "I will kick you out; get out! I'll kick you to death! I loathe all of you!' She attempted to kick Tina, who deftly walked out of the way for her. Nneka went towards her and kept away from the kick targeted at Tina.

'Ugomma,' she said calmly, 'Ugomma. Calm down and come here.'

She shouted, then dropped to her knees and began pounding her face and head violently. She severely wanted to hurt herself. As Ugomma beat her head with her clenched hands, Nneka knelt behind her and grabbed hold of her arms, crossing them in front of her body. She was all the while shouting, screaming and her legs were whipping; however, with her arms encased, she was unable to hurt herself or Nneka. She held her close, so her back was leaning against her chest. The shouting and whipping reached a peak and afterward subsided. They stood by patiently until she was calm, then gradually loosened up her hold. 'Are you okay?' Nneka asked tenderly before she, at last, let go. She nodded, and Nneka turned her round to face her. They were both still on the floor. Her cheeks were red and smudged, and she looked astounded, presumably because they had managed her anger instead of escaping for safety into another room. A moment later, Nneka helped her up, then brought her into the kitchen, where she wiped her face and gave her a drink. She was quiet now, more settled than she'd seen her since she first arrived. Tina returned to the kitchen and asked Ugomma if she would like to play a puzzle with her.

Nneka was astonished at Tina's strength and liberality. She knew that Ugomma's brutal attitude wasn't aimed at her. Personally, Ugomma wanted to pull the entire world down because she was hurting so much, and whoever that stands in her way would get the worst part of her agony. Tina could understand this and be set to overlook and offer friendship and time. Nneka was delighted with her. Tina led her to the cupboard where they found a puzzle bag and went through the garden to amass the puzzle. It didn't take long for Ugomma to get exhausted because of her limited ability to focus, but at least she was encouragingly communicating to Tina, so Tina spread out some paper on the kitchen table and attempted to support her to paint while Nneka made some tea. Ugomma could scarcely hold the paintbrush and couldn't get a handle on the idea of painting an image 'of' something.

'What's that you're painting, Ugomma?' Tina inquired. 'Dark.' 'Is it a sheep or a horse? That looks somewhat like a big horse.' Ugomma didn't respond, focusing on her clumsy project. 'Possibly you could paint the sky with this beautiful brown color?'

'No. Black,' Ugomma said. Notwithstanding Tina's encouragement, Ugomma kept painting only huge, dark splurges, with no enthusiasm for different colors and no clear desire for the painting to represent anything. Nneka had seen this previously; young girls who have been abused and are hurting sometimes only use very dark colors. It's as if their senses have shut down, and they don't see anything about the world around them, so they don't see colors and shapes similarly as other children do. They had their lunch serenely, though it felt more like supper to her, having been up for such a long time.

They had peace all through the evening, and they figured it would be an excellent opportunity to take the photo of Ugomma, which was one of the requirements for the Social Welfare's records. Nneka brought her camera and made her intention known to Ugomma. 'Hope it's okay to take your photo, sweet?' Nneka asked. It was imperative to give Ugomma however much control as could reasonably be expected to ensure her feeling of stability and security. She shrugged, showing her consent. Tina moved aside, so she has only Ugomma in the picture.

She glanced through the lens and framed her head and shoulder against the wall, centering her in the viewfinder.

'Smile,' Ugomma smile,' she said. Ugomma was looking extremely harsh. She saw her mouth pucker to a timid smile, then an arm came up, and she vanished from view. 'Extremely clever, Ugomma. Please, stand still.' Nneka was all the while glancing through the lens. Then her other arm came up and with it her jumper. She put down the camera. 'Ugomma, what's going on with you? Why are you removing your clothes and shoes?' 'Why?' asked Tina, who immediately pulled Ugomma's top back into the right place. She didn't reply. She was moping at them like an ice fish from the freezer, however not glaring, so Nneka immediately snapped the picture and shut the camera. 'Ugomma, it's not proper to take off one's cloth, shoes, or lose your hair for a photograph,' she said. 'For what reason did you do that?' "I want to pull off my clothes. 'I know, darling, but why take them off for a photograph? I didn't ask you to, 'Nneka interfered.

She wasn't going to judge Ugomma's behavior too quickly; however, she needs to put it on her records. Nneka drew out her diary, which the social welfare officer provided for her, and settled down to write everything that had happened so far. The 'log' is a day-by-day record of a child's progress and is something that all guardians keep. It is used to monitor a child's progress and update the social workers, and it's also used as proof during child parenting procedures in court. She had seen child parenting procedures in court before. She was diligent about keeping it up to date since she knew very well how one occurrence could mix into another and how upset evenings could all appear the same sooner or later. The detail was important; just with cautious notes could a pattern of behavior begin to emerge. She made a note of precisely what had occurred: the self-harming in the night and the strange detachment; the lashing out at others and violent tantrums marked by Ugomma's desire to hurt herself; and this abnormal and agitating reaction to having her photograph taken.

"Why had she begun to take her clothes off?

She was unfaltering that she would not hurry into any hasty judgment. Nneka needed to accept Ugomma precisely as she was until further notice and afterward see what originated from her behavior pattern. She was uncomfortable, however, and furthermore thought that it was soothing to write it down. With the other two out for the afternoon, Tina and Nneka took it in turns to engage Ugomma throughout the evening, regardless of this, and for no apparent reason, she threw another full-scale tantrum. She allowed her to continue for a few minutes, hoping it would stop. When it didn't, and the sharp shouting became intolerable, Nneka enfolded her in her arms as she had done previously, until she had calmed down. Afterward, she made another note of Ugomma's whimsical behavior in the record book. She was doing a lot of writing.

Their first weekend with Ugomma was a debilitating and upsetting experience. Albeit none of them said anything, clearly, they were all reasoning something very similar. But it was early days, and they all knew that children could settle down after an initial bout of odd behavior. 'She's a grieved child,' Nneka said to Ukadike when he asked the following day to see how things were going. She informed him about her self-harming and the vicious and forceful fits of rage. 'Truly, that is awful,' said Ukadike. 'It's exceptionally upsetting behavior for such a little child. "Do you think you can cope with her?' 'I'm determined to try,' Nneka said. She just arrived barely one week ago, and I want to give her as much chance as possible.

Furthermore, they realized she was not going to be easy from the beginning, so they can't be astonished if she's a bunch at first. She is keeping detailed notes of everything that happens, however.' 'Good. They'll simply need to observe it and see how it goes. "You're definitely the best individual Ugomma might be with, so as far as you're glad, I know she's in safe hands said Ukadike.' She listened out for Ugomma – she was busy watching a Nickelodeon video – and afterward went through her diary trying to consider something positive to state. 'She eats well, she gorges and needs to limit her intake. She nearly made herself sick yesterday. Aside from having a serious craving, she doesn't have much else going for her at present. 'Do you think she can be contained inside a family?" Ukadike asked his wife. If she can't, the social welfare should start searching for a therapeutic unit, and they're rare. Ukadike had every confidence in her judgment and valued the commendation, but it was little solace. She was already depleted. She was stressed over whether she'd have the ability to see this through and the possibility of falling flat before she'd even begun. She's got contact with Ugomma's parents tomorrow, and her tutor's coming for a few hours tomorrow. Possibly a recognizable face may help settle her. She's been seeing her tutor since September.'

'Alright, Nneka, let's see how it goes. "What are you going to do with her today?' 'Retail therapy," replied Nneka. "Courtesy of Roban Stores.' Ukadike giggled. Ugomma cherished food shopping, unlike the rest of their family, who could think of nothing worse than a trip to the market. She was in her element, pushing the trolley here and there, mentioning to her what they ought to or shouldn't buy. Indeed, she was so eager she needed to constrain her exuberance and return a few things to the shelves. This wasn't uncommon; children of her age regularly appear to feel that an unlimited handbag can solve all their problems. In the homes they had come from, cash was regularly short, and when there was any, it was as often as possible spent on drink, medications, or cigarettes. But she always must be cautious about dealing with their desires, as they could very quickly become demanding and expect they'd be given anything they needed.

Ugomma was a different case, however; from the looks of her luggage and her weight, treats had never been in short supply – which implied that she was accustomed to getting anything she liked. Nneka hoped it wasn't going to be too much of a struggle restricting her to a reasonable limit. However, experience was already teaching her to anticipate a battle. Ugomma picked three packets of cereal at the shopping mall, packets of biscuits and sweets, then said, 'I need them all,' so Nneka was annoyed and started removing things from the trolley as she was putting them in, fully occupied and content. It took almost two hours to finish the weekly shopping. As they finally reached the check-out, Ugomma spotted the display of sweets, tantalizingly positioned along the edge of the aisle. Nneka began emptying the trolley onto the belt and told her to pick a bar of chocolate as a treat since she'd been such a good girl and helped.

Still at the mall, while Nneka was praising her for her conduct throughout the two hours of shopping, Ugomma saw a little girl of about six years old who came for Saturday shopping with her mom and ran after her; she asked the girl to give her the teddy-bear she was having. She refused because of the aggressive way Ugomma requested it. Since the little girl refused to give her the teddy bear, Ugomma started removing her hair and pulling off the little girl's shoe. Her mother separated them, and Nneka ran to the lady and her child to apologize about Ugomma's bad behavior at the mall and vowed never to come to weekend shopping with her.

Nneka asked Ugomma to pick one packet of sweet, 'One,' she repeated, as the packs of sweets began raining into the trolley, her prior cooperation was melting away quickly. "Take the chocolate. Do you like them?" 'Want them all!' she yelled and afterward sat on the floor rebelliously. Some customers' cues behind them were obviously unimpressed by Nneka's parenting aptitudes and shot her one of those looks. Nneka emptied the last of the shopping, including the tom-tom, onto the conveyor and put the other sweets back on the rack. She watched Ugomma out of the corner of her eye. Her annoyance was mounting as she folded her legs, folded her arms, and set her face in a scoff. She kicked the trolley so that it jostled against her side. Nneka held her teeth, pretending that it hadn't hurt. She got the trolley through the walkway and positioned it toward the end, ready to receive the bags of shopping.

Nneka asked her to help her pack their items to their car. 'You were of assistance earlier, and I could do with your help now.' Ugomma refused to make eye contact, and Nneka began to think about how she would move her from the passageway; however, she was determined that she wouldn't get what she needed by making a scene at the shopping mall. Ugomma hollered, 'I don't want those chocolates and sweets,' don't like them?" Nneka looked at her. Don't yell, please, if you don't mind; I have said you can pick one, but hurry up. They've nearly finished, and people are now openly staring at them. Angrily, Ugomma pulled herself quickly to her feet, got a family-sized pack of bubbled sweet, and threw it angrily to the cashier. The sweet hit the innocent woman's face and threw away her eyeglass on the floor, and the lenses shattered.

'Ugomma!' Nneka turned to the cashier, who was looking confusedly and exchanging meaningful looks with other customers. 'I'm so sorry.' apologized Nneka once more, and they left. Outside, she disregarded Ugomma's shouts for the sweets and pushed the trolley quickly towards the car. She opened the door and strapped her under her belt. 'Remain there while I load the bags into the boot. I'm crossed, Ugomma. That was extremely shrewd.' She watched her through the back window. Her jaw was gripped as she mumbled to herself and pounded the seat next to her. She knew how she felt; she was in the mood of thumbing the seat herself. It had been a depleting experience now, and all Nneka could do was set herself up for other hurricanes and hysteria. Yielding to tantrums wouldn't help her or Nneka in the long term. She took the trolley back, then got into the front seat.

'I want the sweets now,' 'Give me the sweets,' Ugomma snarled. I will give you the sweets and chocolates when you've quieted down and apologized. I'm not having that conduct in public.' Ugomma continued yelling, 'Give me them, or I'll poo on your back seat,' she threatened. 'I beg your pardon?" replied Nneka. You certainly will not do that!' So, she thought, she was set to soil herself if she didn't give her precisely what she needed. This was what happened on the first day. Was this her attempting to exert her will rather than nervousness or poor bowel control? While Nneka wasn't ready to surrender to this sort of blackmail, she didn't want her to mess up her back seat. 'Ugomma, if you mess on my back seat intentionally, you won't get any sweets throughout the day. You can't simply make a fuss and get all you want. She is certain Ugomma didn't at her past homes.' I made them,' Ugomma replied. Nneka started the car and pulled towards the exit. She didn't doubt that what she was saying was true. Given Ugomma's shocking behavior, it was no big surprise her previous guardians had surrendered to her requests just to keep her calm. Apparently, this was how she'd acquired the heaps of clothes and toys that she'd arrived with. Ugomma looked through the rear mirror and stuck out her tongue, then began kicking the back of her seat. 'Ugomma, I know it's a hard lesson, yet being naughty won't get you what you need. Just the opposite, in fact.' As they were moving, Ugomma forcefully broke the mirrors at the back seat where she was seated and tried to jump through the window. Was it not for the seat belt holding her, she would've jumped. Few people that saw what was going on flagged Nneka down to stop. She pulled over, Ugomma still attempting to lose the seat belt yet yelling on top of her voice. Nneka got confused about the little girl's attitude. She considered telling Ukadike to take her to the psychiatrist hospital as soon as they got home for a proper examination to ensure she is okay.

'I had all that I wanted at home,' Ugomma said, abruptly more coherent. 'Truly,' Nneka answered, unimpressed. 'I made them, or I'd tell.' 'Tell what, Ugomma? Nneka hesitated. There was a long silence. 'Nothing. Can I have my sweets now, Nneka? I'm sorry. I won't do it again.' 'All right, just as soon as we get home.' As they pulled into the garage, the sour smell from the back seat made her realize that she had made good on her threat. It would be another unwelcome date with the shower for them when they got through the front door.

CHAPTER FIVE

Several weeks later, Ugomma felt safe enough to disclose any more, and during that time, her conduct, far from improving, got even worse. She became progressively violent towards herself, Nneka, and other children. For reasons unknown, she regularly got bothered during dinner. In the middle of a meal, she would suddenly begin mauling at her face or tearing at her hair. On different occasions, she would scratch and squeeze her arms, leaving bruises and wounds. Nneka would quickly restrain her, wrapping her by her arms until she'd calmed down. She was also defecating again. After the first couple of occurrences, she had calmed down and quit messing herself, however now it started up again and was more terrible than before.

Presently she was more violent and just spreading poop all over herself, messing up the chairs, the curtains, and afterward if Nneka didn't get to her rapidly enough, over the house. There was no apparent pattern or motive, but she seemed to understand that destroying fabrics would lead to a more extreme reprimanding than spreading impervious surfaces (for example, the walls or railing), and she seemed to try abstaining from getting it on the couch and curtains. Not surprisingly, it was difficult to understand Ugomma's motives or even whether she was extremely mindful of what she was doing. Because of her activities, the house continually smelled of disinfectant. One night as Nneka prepared for bed, she saw that the skin on her hands had gotten dry and red, and her fingertips were puckered from all the detergents. This habit of Ugomma's was unpleasant for everybody in the house, without a doubt, despite the fact that they had an uncommon tolerance of poor hygiene, having managed various adoptive children with similar issues. Nneka doesn't think she'll ever forget the day she looked around one teenage girl's room, attempting to discover the source of a persistent frightful smell. When she looked behind her closet, she found a stash of used sanitary towels and unwashed underwear dating back to when the teenage girl had first arrived eight months before. Despite the violence, the insults, the excrement, the absence of rest, and various injuries, the god-daughters were remarkably patient with Ugomma, as they now realized that her behavior was not normal.

Not long after the first disclosures, Nneka sat down with them one night, enlightened them regarding the abuse, and cautioned them about some of the additional troublesome conduct they may anticipate. It was important to let them know because Ugomma was as likely to reveal to them as to her, so they needed to be prepared. Moreover, they were already hearing things that Ugomma had begun saying. Similarly, as she had with Uche, she was beginning to drop casual references about what had befallen her into discussions. Nneka needed to tell her goddaughters living with them what she was talking about. With Tina being just thirteen, there were certain physical parts of the abuse that Nneka had to explain to her in detail. When Ugomma mentioned her father weeing in her mouth, for instance, they needed to realize she meant oral sex. Not only was this embarrassing for every one of them, but she was once again reminded of the possible negative impact fostering may be having on any child around. How healthy was it for Tina to learn about sex in this specific circumstance? Was there a risk that it may hurt her relationships in the future? The children were, as she'd anticipated, stunned and horrified. Nneka wished that she hadn't had to bring all this into their worlds as well, and it was dreadful to see them look shocked as they absorbed the implications of what she was saying.

The fact that Ugomma's father had done this to her was obviously an unthinkable and challenging concept for them to adapt to. They have heard many stories about the difficult backgrounds of other children living with abusive parents – for their own safety, they needed to know what had happened – but this was beyond all of that. "As you most likely are aware, this is strictly confidential,' Nneka reminded them, and they nodded at her, their faces serious.

They'd always understood that anything they learned in the house had to stay there and should not be repeated to anyone. She confided in them totally. After they had this conversation, the children became considerably more tolerant of Ugomma's behavior. They tried to spend more time playing with Ugomma and remain compassionate even when she was shouting at them to "Get out of my fucking house!" or jumping at them with a kick. Nevertheless, their understanding had limits. One day during dinner, Ugomma interfered by graphically recounting how her finger was cut by her mom intentionally, and blood had dribbled from it. Kate became irritated. 'Gosh!' she shouted, then she picked her plate with her dinner and moved to the living room.

One evening, when Ugomma had been with them for about eight months, Chioma came around for one of their regular meetings. She is a social worker, and good practice directed that she comes around each four to six weeks to check how things were going, offer a bit of help, and check Nneka's report notes. As it was a glorious bright day, they chose to take Ugomma to the recreation center. Despite having been up most of the night with bad dreams and general distress, as she frequently seemed to be, Ugomma was brimming with energy and fretful to get out into the daylight. Nneka, then again, was basically exhausted. 'So, how's she doing?' asked Chioma, as they strolled through the recreation center's flawlessly tended flower garden.

Ugomma was walking a few meters ahead, anxious to get to the playing area, and obviously unaware of the great cluster of colors and aromas around her. 'She's getting worse, 'Nneka answered. 'She's having more and more of those crazy screaming fits, for no obvious reason, and once she recovers, she appears to be aware of what's happened. That's the reason Uche didn't stay for the mentoring this morning; about once a week, Ugomma simply is unmanageable, so they have to give up and cancel the session.' 'And how's she sleeping?' 'Not wonderfully. She awakens at five, at times earlier. She had been learning how to remain in her room and play discreetly. But over a couple of weeks, she's begun having horrendous bad dreams, which appear to be more like hallucinations. They're real to her, and in some cases, they seem to continue after she's woken up. It's dreadful; they wake up to her shouting, screaming, and find her squirming on the floor, then she likes that off and on for the rest of the night.

Nneka keeps a seat outside her room at some point, so once she has settled her the first time, she simply stays there waiting. If she is fortunate, she gets the opportunity to snooze for a couple of moments until she starts up again!' 'You should be totally shattered," said Chioma. They arrived at the play area, where Ugomma bounced on a swing and began working herself ever higher. 'Watch out, Ugomma,' Nneka cautioned, then stood with Chioma on the grass verge, where Ugomma could see her watching. She had no feeling of danger or instinct to protect herself and would swing out of control, then tumble off, if allowed to. 'How did the hearing test go?' Chioma inquired. Nneka had taken Ugomma for a test earlier that week, as there had been occasions when she didn't appear to hear what was happening around her.

'I believe it's OK, ' replied Nneka. We're hanging tight for the doctor's letter, yet the medical attendant assumed there was nothing wrong with her.' 'So, she is shut down?' asked Chioma, alluding to the way some gravely abused children seem to switch off their senses as a method of protecting themselves. If you can't see, hear, or feel anything, it probably won't be happening. When they shut down in this manner, these children become less mindful of what's happening around them and less aware of things that they generally take for granted, such as noticing the pleasant taste of food or recognizing that the water in the shower is excessively hot.

'I suspect as much,' she replied. 'There are undoubtedly signs. Practically nothing gives her any delight. She doesn't appear to be sensitive to temperature: even when it was freezing, Nneka needed to battle with her consistently to stop her from wearing only a T-shirt and shorts. There are days when she is on a relatively even keel, she assumes; however, she cannot depict even those as good days. If they manage to get through a day without a full-scale tantrum, they've done amazingly well. That seldom happens.' Chioma looked at her sympathetically. 'You're working extremely hard; I realize that. You're doing a splendid job; you truly are, she said.' Nneka grinned feebly. Praises were nice, yet what she truly needed was a good night's rest. She was continually depleted, and although her patience was just about lasting out, she felt at the end of her tether. They began strolling back, satisfied that the outing had so far gone without incident. The sun was still bright, but she was quick to capitalize on Ugomma's good conduct. If they could return home without any drama, it would permit her to praise and reward her, and they could set a positive point of reference for how a day out should go. Chioma and Nneka each took one of Ugomma's hands as they strolled back through the recreational center. 'She is so worried about the absence of any improvement,' she said, using deliberately vague language so that Ugomma wouldn't understand that they were discussing her. 'The disturbances are getting worse, particularly at night.' 'And have any of the disclosures dealt with the maternal presence as they talked about?' 'No. She tells her about those events repeatedly, but there's not really any new information coming out.

Frankly, Nneka is worried; things appear to be getting worse rather than better. Is there no helpful advice you can give me?" said Nneka. She tried to keep the edge of desperation from her voice. 'No more than you're already doing,' Chioma said thoughtfully. 'And to be honest, there's a limit to what you ought to be expected to adapt to. It's possible that the emotional trauma is extreme to the point that only a therapeutic unit can put it right. Chioma promised to check and see what's available. She won't do anything; she'll simply have a look.' As they arrived at the corner of her road, she permitted Ugomma to run ahead while Chioma and Nneka walked peaceful-ly. She had been hoping for some practical advice, but the degree of Ugomma's disturbance seemed to be out-side Chioma's experience too. Nneka was disappointed, but she vowed to press on.

On their way back, Ugomma had stopped further up and was hunching with her back to her, carefully focused on something in the gutter. 'What's going on with you, Ugomma? Nneka called. Come here. "She turned around, smiling, then held up a dead bird on the one hand and a liquid-like substance, on the other hand, gladly showing it as a trophy to both Chioma and Nne-ka. The liquid substance was black in color and had a foul smell coming out from it while the bird's head dropped sideways, and its breast had been torn open so that its bloody internal organs were exposed. Inside that gutter, too, was a dead cat. Ugomma glared at it, captivated and smiling as if to say she has won an American lottery. 'Ugomma! Put that down, right now!' Nneka said resolutely. She stared at her, then gradually turned away, poking at the bird's bloody flesh, and dropped it back in the gutter. 'Chim ooo,' Chioma gasped. Nneka cupped Ugomma's elbows in her hands from behind and steered her, arms outstretched, towards the house. Chioma got straight in her vehicle without coming in, as she had another meeting to attend. Nneka moved Ugomma in through the front door and directly to the kitchen sink. She looked up at her as she filled the bowl with hot water and soap.

'We had a nice time at the park, didn't we, Nneka?' Her face was flushed, more joyful than she'd seen her in weeks. Nneka grinned back. She couldn't be annoyed; after all, she hadn't really done anything wrong. But she was worried at the ghoulish fascination the dead bird had inspired. The following morning it was evident early that something was different. Ugomma wasn't shouting at five o'clock, nor six, nor seven. Nneka had the opportunity to shower, dress and dry her hair. She made the children's packed snacks and even drank some coffee in harmony. Then she started to worry about Ugomma. She crawled up the steps, tiptoed to Ugomma's door, and listened. There was silence. She wasn't talking to herself as usual, which she often does, even in her quieter moment. She knocked and went in. She was lying on top of the duvet, flat on her back, with her eyes wide open, gazing at the roof. She was still like that for a second; Nneka dreaded she could be dead.

'Ugomma!' she shook her shoulder. 'Ugomma!' She gave a slight twitch at the corner of her eye. 'Ugomma!! What's wrong? Are you ill?' She didn't move. Her arms and legs were held straight, so hardened it was like they were encased in concrete. Nneka knew this wasn't a fit, or at least not like any fit she had ever observed. She placed her palm on her forehead. It was warm and not feverish. 'Ugomma!! Can you hear me?' she shook her once more, this time more vigorously. 'Ugomma, look at me. Tell me what's going on with you. It's Nneka. Ugomma, can you hear me?' She winked, then gradually turned to look at her. Her pupils were enlarged, and there were large dark rings around her eyes. Ugomma opened her mouth and spoke in a flat monotone. "I saw him here last night. You promised he wouldn't, yet he did." I know, I know who it was.' Nneka knelt down and held her hand tight. 'No sweet, nobody came here. She asked if she had remembered something that appeared to be real.'

'They asked me not to tell. I didn't tell them because they said I would turn to a zombie if I do.' 'Somebody saw Daddy do ill-disciplined things to you?" asked Nneka. She gestured. 'Who, sweet? Who was it?' She glared directly at her, eyes wide with fear, her cheeks deathly pale. She could see the agony of an abused child in her face. "Mommy. Mommy saw. I pleaded with her to make him stop; however, she didn't. She giggled and watched. They all did.' Nneka turned cold." 'They?" asked Nneka. There were others there?' 'Uncle Bennett, and Ken, and Aunt Liz. They took pictures when Uncle Mikel did it.' 'Uncle Mikel?' Her face was clear, she was looking at Nneka and talking, but it was like she was in a daze. 'He lay on me, same as Daddy. I didn't want it because it hurt a lot. I struggled to get up, I struggled to shout at the top of my voice, but they overpowered me. Daddy held me when it was Uncle Mikel's turn. I was screaming and shouting, so Daddy put his thing in my mouth. Auntie Liz is wicked sometimes; she said, "That will quiet her down." And they all giggled.' Ugomma was shaking with dread.

Nneka attempted to shroud her shock and focus on what she was hearing. She needed to ensure she recalled all the names and details to get as much proof as possible while Ugomma was talking. She didn't have any idea when she would open up again. Nneka stroked her forehead and murmured words of comfort. 'Ugomma, you're protected at this point. The doors are bolted and locked. We have a perfect alarm; nobody can get in," said Nneka. What they did was a terrifying thing any grown-up can do to a kid. They are all wicked, Ugomma.' She nodded, yet without conviction. 'They gave me lots of sweets and toys.' She looked at the flooding toy boxes. 'Did they purchase all these?' Nneka inquired. She nodded once more. So that's what they were – not presents, not things intended to bring joy; they were bribes, to buy silence and deference. No wonder they don't mean anything to you. 'Ugomma, good adults don't buy children presents because they've done terrible things to them. Was it to stop you telling?'

'It was our secret. They said if I told, horrifying things would happen to me. That I'll be taken to a dark cave and a beast would come and bite off my arms. Will he, Nneka?' Her voice rose frightfully. 'Will he come here and chomp off my arms or kill me?' 'No, absolutely not,' Nneka replied. Those people are the only monsters, and they won't come anywhere close to you, ever again," Nneka assured. She considered this, and afterward, a sad smile crossed her lips. 'Aunt Liz was nice. She didn't do things" She just watched.' Nneka shivered at this twisted logic. 'That's bad too, Ugomma. She watched you being harmed and didn't help. She ought to have stopped them. That's what I would have done. Where were they when they were viewing? Asked Nneka. 'In my room," Ugomma answered. 'And the car? She once said something regarding a car? Who was in the car, Ugomma?' 'Mommy and Daddy. Mommy took the photos of Daddy and me. It's a huge car. We were at the back. It was dark. I don't like the dark. The camera made it light up. Will he be reprimanded, Nneka? 'I genuinely hope so, sweet," Nneka answered. Every one of them. I'll tell your social worker, and she'll tell the police. The police will need to talk to us but don't worry, I'll be with you," said Nneka.' She was all the while holding her hand and stroking her forehead, hesitant to let go. It was well after seven, and she should have been waking the others for school. 'Is there something else you need to reveal to me now? Nneka asked. You've been very bold, and it's important you let me know if there is.' Ugomma shook her head. Nneka snuggled her for a while, then tenderly eased her into bed and tried to focus her mind.

'Nneka?' she said abruptly. 'Yes, sweet?' 'Is my father a good man? Nneka said no, he is evil by hurting an innocent child. He will soon be in police custody and be punished accordingly alongside his accomplices for their evil deeds. 'Did your daddy do those things to you?' 'No. Absolutely not,' Nneka said. 'Never in a million years. He's a decent, kind man. Most adults are.' 'And Tina and Kate's daddy?' 'No. Tina's daddy never hurt her. Kate's daddy hit her, which is the reason she's here. Yet, he didn't hurt her like that.'

'Are you sure it's not my fault, Nneka? "No, she replied."

"Mommy said I was fortunate because daddy likes me so much that's why he treats me that way. She said I should belt up and appreciate it. She said I was Daddy's girl.' 'She wasn't right, Ugomma. Parents snuggle their kids to show their affection. They don't hurt them. And it wasn't your flaw, Ugomma. Don't you ever accept that" Nneka gave her another embrace, then she requested for the television, and for the first time since arriving, she seemed to remain in bed while the others were up. Nneka left her room and stood for a moment on the landing, attempting to pull it together. She was super cold and shuddering with rage. She could see Ugomma being held down by her father. She could see the others watching. She could hear their chuckling. It was amazing she was stable. She knew now where her fury had originated from, and she presently shared it. She had no desire to trust it could be any worse than Ugomma's father exposing her to the vile acts she had described, but now, sadly, she understood it was a whole lot more terrible than anyone had suspected. She had been the casualty of the most dreadful sort of abuse she could envision. Where not only one of her parents subjected her to the most corrupting treatment any child could endure, but where both were complicit, and so were other adults.

Nneka could feel the queasiness churning in her as she understood that it was not only her parents, in their position of precious care and trust, but many others who had schemed to turn Ugomma's world into a nightmare of affliction and perversion. They had overturned everything that ought to be good in a child's life, transforming it into something so profoundly devilish and evil that Nneka couldn't find the words to quantify what she thought of it. No wonder Ugomma had cut off the world around her and had no sense of relating to other people when all she had encountered was agony, cruelty, and pain. No surprise, she attempted to beat herself, disfigure herself, and smeared herself with poop – what else had she ever known? Somehow Nneka made breakfast and saw Tina and Kate off to class.

When they were gone, she phoned Chioma and disclosed everything to her. 'It's more terrible than we suspected,' she said. 'Much more awful.' As Nneka reported what Ugomma had said, she could detect Chioma taking in the size of what had occurred. She breathed in sharply as she told her that Ugomma had been abused by a circle of complicit adults, photographed, and watched and jeered at. 'Gracious Lord, Nneka." She couldn't believe what that child has been through. This should be enough for police to arrest them,' she said. 'She realized it must have been horrific to hear all this from her; however, you've done a great job.' "I didn't feel like I'd done a good job," replied Nneka. She felt as though she'd been involved with Ugomma's anguish. She felt embarrassed to be grown-up. 'Can we figure out how long this has been going on?' Chioma asked. 'Quite a while, I think Nneka replied. Ugomma asked if her own father did it to her and was astonished to hear he didn't. The way she describes it, it sounds like it was the norm, daily occurrence, and it's only now she realizes it's wrong.' Nneka stopped. 'Chioma, at what age can a child be assaulted?' 'Any age; there are cases as young as six months." Nneka winced. 'Nneka, this has all the signs of a pedophile ring. Was she at any point shown the photographs?' 'Not as far as she is aware. She didn't say.' 'OK, record everything when you have a chance.

Chioma guaranteed her she will speak to the appropriate authority so that they will take it up. They'll want a forensic medical and a police memorandum interview; then, she'll get back to her. All were in the past, and Nneka now lives alone with her husband and Chizoba.

CHAPTER SIX

Nneka and her husband loved Chizoba so much due to her hardworking nature. Despite her little age, she still wakes up before any soul and arranges everything in the house. She would sweep the general compound, scrub the flat they lived in, wash plates, and warm the food. Even the neighbors were beginning to love her due to her respectful nature. Waking up the next day, her aunt, whom she addresses as her City mom, was standing at the door of her room wearing a pretty smile. Chizoba greeted her, and she responded; she was asked to go get prepared that they would be heading out. "Where could she possibly want to take her to," Chizoba wondered. She hurriedly said her morning prayers and quickly went to the bathroom, where she brushed and had her bathe. She came out beautifully dressed; her aunt had bought her clothes a day ago. Nneka smiled when she saw how pretty she was looking and decided to halt the suspense. "Today, I will be taking you for sightseeing; we will be touring today so you can see other fun places in the town," she said.

Chizoba was so happy to hear that. She had always wanted to visit many places and see those things she had heard in the village. They both got prepared and left. Nneka and Chizoba decided to use the commercial bus. The bus which they boarded dropped them at the City's amusement park. They alighted from the bus, and Chizoba seeing the magnificent building, was in total awe and wondered what some of those were. They moved to the amusement park and there she saw many children, some with their parents while some alone, they were all having fun and she couldn't wait to join the activities.

There she saw what looked like a bird flying up. She also saw little children, cars lined up rotating at full speed while the children sitting there were laughing while some were screaming. Those screaming were those who happened to ride in it for the first time.

"Do you want to try one of those?" her aunt asked, and she quickly nodded her head in excitement that shows she wanted to. They hopped in and were told to hold on tight as it kicked off. Every normal City girl hopping on those cars would definitely scream on their first day, but in the case of Chizoba, it was the reverse. Instead of screaming when it started rotating and moving at high speed and mileage, she laughed heavily, even her aunt was a bit scared, but Chizoba enjoyed every bit of it. She tried all sorts of fun activities in the amusement park.

She was allowed to play with other children who carried her along while her aunt was watching. By the end of the day, they went back home, and Chizoba was overjoyed. Her aunt had promised to take her to ride on a boat the next day. The next day was the D-day for the boat touring. It was about 7:01 am when her aunt came knocking. "Knock- knock."

"Chizoba," her aunt called,

"It's seven o'clock, wake up my dear...!

"Oh, thanks to God," Chizoba replied.

She stood up from bed and observed her daily routine and obligation, though prayers are perceived as a mandatory requirement of every man. She said her morning prayers, and after then, she picked up the broom at the back of her door, swept the compound and the rooms, dressed her bed, washed her face, and brushed her teeth. She ran to her aunt. "Good morning, mom." "How are you?" her aunt asked.

"I'm fine, mom," she said and looked for her City dad (Nneka's husband) but couldn't find him. She asked about him, and her aunt explained to her that he had left for work. Ukadike is a businessman who trades in Onitsha main market. Onitsha main market is the biggest market in the eastern region of Nigeria. Chizoba knew that there was more to see and know about Onitsha.

"Zoba (like she would fondly call Chizoba), my daughter, let's have our breakfast, but before that, go and have your bath while I proceed to the kitchen," her aunt said. She ran to the bathroom as fast as she could, took her bath, and applied some lotion then got dressed. "Mom, I'm done," she said while going to the kitchen in search of her City mom. On Getting to the kitchen, her aunt had finished preparing breakfast. Her aunty called on her from the dining. "Sit, let's eat," she said. She was amazed to behold the delicious meal before her.

"This must be very delicious," she thought and shook her head

"Dear, eat up; we have a long way to go," said her aunt. It was so obvious that she couldn't stop staring at the meal with smiles. She was holding well-cooked noodles with fried eggs garnished with carrot and green beans, a glass of fruit juice, not like her normal regular village meals. "My dear, eat," her aunt cut in.

Mrs. Nneka stood up after eating and went to her room, coming out with a big black sack bag. "My dear, when u are done eating take this back to your room and change to something else," her aunt told her. Having food in her mouth, Chizoba nodded her head in response.

"Mom, thanks for the food; it was indeed a palatable and delicious meal which differs from the village meal," Chizoba complimented. "All thanks to God for provision," her aunty quickly replied. Chizoba took the dish to the kitchen and got them washed; she took the bag given to her by her aunty to her room. She was amazed at seeing the new outfit her aunt got her again. She quickly changed into something else, just as her aunt demanded. "This is beautiful indeed," she said. She came out looking pretty, and then her journey to the wonder river (like she would always call river Niger) set. Chizoba and her aunty boarded a motorcycle from the house and got to a particular bus stop located at old road Onitsha;

they waited for ten minutes. Then the bus heading to Asaba head Bridge (Asaba is the capital city of Delta state Nigeria) stopped, and they hopped in. Chizoba was taking a tour with her eye, looking at the big four-story buildings. This city is indeed a township (township is a common word used to address the city, mainly in Igbo land). Her aunt said to her, “My daughter, look, this is the army gate. From here, you will get to the barracks, which is the soldiers’ camp,” she explained. Chizoba kept on nodding her head in response. Getting to the next bus stop, Nneka pointed towards the right, turned, and said

“Chizoba here is called Upper Iweka (a big park sited at Onitsha). This the last bus stop for all the vehicles coming from Lagos, Abuja, and all other states in the country to Anambra. But my dear, it’s equally a bad area for travelers; people get robbed here and sometimes get killed.” Chizoba overwhelmed in fear, grabbed her aunt’s hand and held her close. She didn’t utter a word. Her aunt said to her when they got to the last bus stop, “We are stopping here, my dear.” “That’s the Niger Bridge,” she pointed to her. “Wow, it’s so big, mom” “Look right and left; it’s river Niger,” her aunt said to her. “Mom, look at this big car,” Chizoba exclaimed. “It’s called a luxury bus,” aunty Nneka explained.” “Mom, look at this car, Okwuoto Ekene Eze. “Nneka laughed and replied to her,

"It's called a Jeep; Okwuoto Ekene Eze is too local. (Okwuoto Ekene Eze is a name used to refer to a Jeep car mainly in the timid part of Igbo land.) "Let's go down to the riverbank," her aunt said to her.

Getting down to the riverbank, Chizoba was so amazed and felt like swimming, but the river was too big. Chizoba looked at her aunt and said to her.

"Mom, the river is so big and large (stretching her hands in demonstration). "It's not like mmiri Amaokpala in our village. Mom, can I touch it?" "Yes, dear, but wait, let's get a boat." Her aunt called one of the canoe paddlers who toured them all through. They navigated from Onitsha to Asaba. While on the boat, strange sounds emanated from the depth of the river. Chizoba wondered what that could be. "It might be the river goddess or the fishes, but this sounds like that of the river goddess," the sailor explained to her. The sailor told her how so many lives got missing inside the river. Fear gripped Chizoba, and she demanded they turn back, but the sailor told her they were almost at Adams.

"Here we are, my dear," the sailor said.

"But mom, where are the fishes?" Chizoba asked. "It is towards that endpoint forward, that's where the Fishermen gather to fish, but it's sunny; the fishes are deep down the sea; fishing starts before the sun sets," the sailor answered. "Yes, I know," Chizoba replied, nodding her head. Let's return, her aunt demanded, but Chizoba wanted to swim.

"Mom, please, can I swim in it?" "No, my dear, it's too deep for you," her aunt told her. "Yes, I know, but I used to swim in the Amaokpala River," she said reluctantly. Her aunt laughed and replied to her, "Dear, not today its 4:30 pm already; let's get going." They went home for the day. Chizoba was so happy and wished she could share her experience with her friends back in the village, mainly to Nnedi. It was indeed an awesome experience for her. Chizoba was enrolled in secondary school at the age of eleven. It was indeed an added bonus to her. Nobody who knows her family would ever believe such due to their poor condition, but here she is, attending the City's best school. Thanks to Nneka and Ukadike. Even Chizoba thought the happenings to be a mere imagination, but the pain she felt on pinching herself speaks volumes of an unbound reality. Urban Community Secondary School, by standard, is a very reputable school in town. It has the credit of having produced many influential individuals in every sector of the country - senators, rep members, chairmen, ministers, and three past Presidents. The school has a very gigantic and magnificent look. The school library is even bigger than some schools.

Chizoba could not really believe her eyes on her first day in school. She had never seen a school as big as her current school in her whole life. It differed totally from her school in the village. Though her village school was built by the white missionaries, it was just a hall that was demarcated by standing boards, with each space serving as classes for different levels. "Nzu" was being used at times in place of chalk, and the pupils all had their slates with which they wrote on. Here, a big mansion is being used to run a school with whiteboards that have its own pen (marker). Oyibo magic, she smiled to herself. Her mind wandered back to her village. No single building in the village could compare to her school in beauty; even the village palace was nowhere close.

"I know Igwe Atikpa would even love to work as a gatekeeper here just to behold this very mansion on a daily basis," she said. "Who is Igwe Atikpa?" a voice came from behind. Chizoba was covered in shock. Such a state of shock wouldn't have been invented if she knew she had been talking out all this while. Who is this girl, and could she read people's minds? She reasoned, recovering from her sudden shock. On noticing the scenario, the little girl decided to break the silence.

"I'm Christabel, so sorry for intruding, but is he your father?" the little girl questioned.

"No! He is our village king," Chizoba muttered.

"Okay, I thought as much because I know him, and besides, my mom didn't tell me any of my cousins were coming to this school" "Igwe Atikpa is my uncle, though I have not seen him before, I have heard much about him; Is he as wicked as my mom do say?" "This is strange, "Chizoba whispered under her breath. This mysterious child that just succeeded some minutes ago in reading her mind is now searching for a tender Palm fruit in her mouth. What if she was sent on a mission by some mischievous fellas to bring her down? "Is anything the matter?" Christabel questioned, awakening her from her thought.

"No! He is our village king," she exclaimed. "I know; you have told me that already. Are you bored by something dear, you are acting strange, or are you still homesick? "No way, I don't need the service of a soothsayer to tell me she is a witch, " Chizoba concluded in her mind. If not, why would she know I'm missing my mother, and who is your dear? "I am alright, and if you don't mind, I'd like to be left alone; just not in a mood to answer questions this early morning," she spoke out in a more polished English. Even though she never traveled, she could speak to the admiration of anyone. She put in the effort to learn from the whites that once stayed in her village. Christabel came to love her the more owing to her polished accent. As they were still conversing, a bell rang thrice, and within a matter of seconds, students were seen trooping from different directions to a particular direction.

"I have to go now, "appealed Christabel.

"What is that bell for, and why are people such in a hurry?" asked Chizoba.

"That's for the morning assembly," she replied, already gone.

Chizoba looked at the wristwatch her new mother had bought her, and surprisingly it was still 7:25 am. Remembering her village school again, she gave out a heavy smile. Nobody would be in that school by now except for those who had come in mufti to sweep their mango leave-filled compound. The kind of orderliness being maintained still seemed strange to her. Back in her village school, it would take both the intervention of the headmaster's "utali," a long cane and the continuous beating of the big car wheel, which served as a bell, to get the students assembled for the morning assembly; before finally saying the Lord's prayer by 8:30 am and sometimes 9 o'clock. Even the teachers are in the habit of coming late as some will have to go to the market to sell their farm produce before proceeding to school. She made an imagery of the village headmaster, with his bald head and protruding stomach, equipped with two or more "utalis" in his hands, running around the classrooms, beating, and shouting "onuku" to anyone he finds in the classroom. This made her laugh so hard. She could remember the very day she was unfortunate.

She had gone to school as early as 8 o'clock on that fateful day and was sitting in the classroom wholly engulfed in her assignment that the continuous oozing of the bell made no meaning to her. As is already a habit, students never take any assignment seriously until the night before or early morning on the day of submission; then you will see them blinking like a thief and searching for whose assignment to copy. As she was busy perfecting her work, behold the bald man running towards her with enormous anger drawn in his face. On sighting him, her heart jumped out of her body, knowing it's already a bad day for her and there was no escape route. Ask for a beating monger, and you will be shown the man standing right before her.

"Oya, Onuku, co...co...co...co...come here osiso," he stammered, sweating profusely with his half-tucked shirt on baggy trousers and his big short tie. His tie can comfortably serve as a scarf for a big-headed woman.

On approaching him, she was welcomed with a hard resounding knock that sent vibration down her spine, leaving her whole body in a fidgeting motion. "You are very stupid for being in the right place at the wrong time. What are you doing here by this time? Oya leg down fast!" He thundered in command.

"It's already 9:15 am, and you are still here shaking your small bum bum." Everyone knows that Mr. Ojo's questions are always rhetoric and would surely be accompanied by "Leg Down," his most favorite words. Despite his contentiousness, students still love him the most, for he is not just funny all the time but has his own slang that students do love to hear. Leg down, a slang meaning to kneel, is the most popular of them all. So popular that it had gained him a famous nickname, such that whenever Mr. Leg down is mentioned anywhere, even the deaf and dumb fellows know it is the headmaster. Chizoba knelt down and was given the beating of her life.

"Oya, rush to the assembly and always remember to give your testimony to anyone still hanging around that was opportune to come your way," he yelled. In a Usain Bolt-like manner, she speedily zoomed off to the assembly ground with tears still in her eyes. Mr. Ojo has a zigzag pattern of flogging. He beats you all over the body. From a knock on the head to beatings on the hands, on the back, on the buttocks, on the leg, and then he repeats the process twice more. Whether you are crying or not is none of his business. One thing about him was the fact that he never fails to finish what he had started. The fun of it all is that he never ceases to make you laugh, even when he's punishing you for an offense. Any given stroke of the cane is accompanied by the phrase, "Jesus loves you," in which you give an "Amen" as a reply. Any contrary saying or silence will only attract a minus.

That was indeed an experience she would never forget all her life and one that really transformed her for good. She hurriedly followed the direction Christabel had gone.

Each student was dressed in their neatly ironed uniform. Nneka had helped her to iron her blue pinafore and white shirt the previous day. The senior girls wore white shirts on blue skirts, with a well-knotted tie and blue beret, while the boys wore white shirts on blue trousers with ties and a neat haircut. The junior boys had the same dress, save the fact that they had on shorts instead of trousers, and the junior girls had pinafore instead of a skirt. All went on marching with white shoes. Mr. Williams, the principal of Urban Community Secondary School, without much ado, mounted the podium and started addressing the mammoth student crowd. All thanks to the Omniscient. The author and giver of life for once again making this assemblage a possibility after a long-term break. Once more, we give him the accrued glory. The Urban Community Secondary School is undoubtedly the most reputable among its equals, having been subdued to the test of time and still victorious par excellence. A new session we have entered, a new season we have begun.

It's indeed a new phase of life for the JSS One students in particular and to us all in general, who have come to dine from the banquet of knowledge and quench their hallowed academic thirst by drinking from the meritorious pot of Wisdom. An Urbanite can never be intimidated anywhere he finds himself, for we not only give a drink but allow a swim voyage to the Solomonian adventurer quest. This is wholesomely evident with our gigantic Library, which is the largest in the whole wide City without an iota of doubt.

Your parents have sent you to spend this wonderful six years of your life with us, as a prerequisite to making them proud in the future and becoming better of yourselves and better individuals in society. The saying that "an Urbanite is naturally ahead of you" is no joke, for we have succeeded in giving and continuously giving better seeds to the populace. We have Senators, House of representative members, ministers, clergymen of repute, Doctors, Lawyers, and Engineers, and so on to our credit. To crown it all, we have given this nation three Presidents, an unprecedented achievement in any school's history. I am not a prophet, but I see bright futures even as I face this crowd today. Many among you will climb the echelon of high offices in the future, which will only be possible by determination and focus, which is an individualistic factor. Likewise, some will descend to the point of regret later in life. God forbid evil, but that's the reality of life. We must forever be mindful of the fact that bad company corrupts good manners and that despite the company, we are on an individual race. Many of us come on different missions but in all we do, bear it in mind that a failure is never celebrated, and as such, all your actions must be success-perforated.

Congratulations to the five of our last set SS3 students that emerged glorious in the Elizabethan exams. They are currently chilling in different institutions abroad. To me, that should be the dream of any well-meaning student. Though a hard task it is to achieve success but today, I equip you all with the double-edged sword of focus and determination as the sure requirement to become victorious in the arduous battle of success. In all, remember to always pray for grace, for hard work without grace is nothing but an effort in futility. We encourage our old students to always be of good behavior, and as is our tradition, any defaulter is sure pricing an expulsion ticket. We are the best, and the best will continue being our trademark of honor.

I am your father and a transparent and approachable fellow, so feel free to bring your burdens to me. And never fail to report any mischievous fellow; report any reportable, be it students or your teachers. Your anonymity is assured, and you will be satisfied with the way the issue will be handled. Remember, we frown so rudely at cultism and do not take it lightly with anyone that indulges in such acts. Always desist from bad company, and you will be my friend. To our day students, let punctuality be your hallmark, and I promise we all will happily, smoothly, and gently perambulate on this academic exploration. "Thank you, and always be of good behavior." A thunderous clap ensued immediately, and the principal finished his speech. It was such an invigorating one. Mr. Williams is indeed a known orator. His oratory experience has taken him far and wide. In fact, he was made the President of the Association of City Principals (AOCP) due to his speech prowess. In all, he's a dedicated fellow and always wore a radiantly soothing smile.

Chizoba liked the speech a whole lot. Her aim in life has always been to make mama proud, and here she is, presented with an eagle opportunity. "... many among you are going to climb the echelon of high offices in the future, and this will only be possible by determination and focus, which is an individualistic factor," the principal's voice keeps echoing and re-echoing to her. "I will succeed!" She said in a prayer-like manner as if being interviewed by an unseen spirit. Students have now retired to their various classes for the day's activities. What marvels her was the programmed nature of every event; despite the principal's long harangue, the assembly took just fifteen minutes, with none of the items in the assembly manual skipped. Her village school never had any manual for assembly.

"Maybe because it's a primary school," she thought.

During the break, Chizoba decided to stay behind and recap what they had been taught so far. "Guess who we have here?" a familiar voice came from behind.

On turning back, it was Christabel. In an involuntary-like manner, Chizoba rushed and hugged her. Although she never seemed to like the mind reader initially, she seemed to be the only friend she had now in the whole school. "Are you in this class, too?" asked Christabel. "Yes, "she answered, happiness building up gradually in her." Wow, how come I didn't notice you in class all this while; I really like this development, at least we are going to know more about each other if you wish. Can we be friends?" she asked frantically. "We are already friends," answered Chizoba. "I know, but for formality's sake. So can we be friends?" I'm beginning to like this fellow the more, Chizoba thought to herself. It was barely a few hours ago that they came to know each other, and here she is, giving out a behavior that suggests they have known each other for over a decade. What an extrovert. Chizoba, on her own, is a renowned extrovert; she can really talk for Africa. Here are two talkative trying to augment.

"Yes, we can be friends," she replied.

They hugged again in celebration of their newfound friendship. Chizoba packed her book inside the locker, and both started heading to the school canteen to seal their newbie coagulation. "So, can you tell me more about yourself? "Chizoba inquired. "Well, I don't really know the aspect you wish to know about me, but I think my name is of utmost importance. I'm Uwadiegwu Christabel Chiemerie, though my friends call me UCC for short. What about you?" Chizoba had gone back to her thinking state; what on earth is really happening here? Here is a girl she met in a way that she's yet to discern, and she's now bearing her surname. Is this a joke, or its kind? Had it been she had said her own name; she would have concluded that she was mimicking or making jest of her. Or had she employed her magical antics on her again? What marveled her the most was the fact that she claimed to know the man that happens to be her community king, saying he's even her uncle. Does this in any way suggest she is also from Amaokwu, her village? But the king doesn't answer her surname, and to the best of her knowledge, she's not in any way related to the royal family; and surname is usually peculiar to people of the same paternal antecedent. Something is wrong somewhere and not so far from this hysterical young lass.

"I'm Chizoba," she said.

"A nice name it is, though an addendum of a Christian name or better still a surname would have been more official."

"Oh, pardon my manners. My name in full is Uwadiegwu Caroline Chizoba."

"Wow, what a coincidence, though mine is more original," she jokingly said.

"I think I need to sue you for plagiarizing my name," Chizoba retorted. They both laughed hysterically. In the canteen, they bought some biscuits and minerals and were really getting cool with each other. Despite the seeming intimacy, Chizoba still had about hundred-dollar questions roaming her mind about who Christabel really was. On the other hand, Christabel was quite happy about everything and was obviously not thinking in that direction. One would easily mistake the duo to be twins because, despite the fact that they looked alike, they also bore the same surname and from the same village, and by coincidence, happened to be in the same JSS1C and were of equal height. The only distinguishing factor remained the fact that Christabel was fairer in complexion.

"Are you both twins?" A teacher had asked them.

"Yes, from different mothers," Christabel had chipped in.

"Wow, what a striking resemblance," he said.

Many people indeed thought them to be twins, and both seemed inseparable as the day passed, gaining more admiration from their folks.

CHAPTER SEVEN

The joy Chizoba had the very day her City Mom gave birth knew no bound. At least her prayer had been answered. On several occasions, she remembered her in prayer; and now here she is, blessed with a bouncing baby boy and girl.

"Beautiful children," she said, looking at them with her face covered with smiles." What if God had given aunt Nneka her own children as she had once prayed?" she reasoned and laughed sheepishly. She remembered the very day she was praying and crying in the church for God to bless her aunt. If not for anything, at least for the known fact that she and her husband had been good to her. After witnessing her aunt receive an insult from a woman in the market, Chizoba, full of sorrow, had gone to church that same evening to intercede for her on her own will.

She had prayed:

"Oh Heavenly Father, the maker of heaven and earth. You established your kingdom in the highest peak and have the earth as your stepping stool. You are everywhere and see everything as I was made to understand. You know our intentions even before we pour them out to you in prayers. I come to you this very day with a heavy-laden heart. Please have mercy on my aunt; bless her with her own children and save her from all these gruesome insults and shame associated with childlessness. I don't exactly know what she had done to you, but I plead you to forgive her. Even if she's meant to be barren, please Lord, open her womb. And if possible, take some of my unborn children and give them to her.........

This was exactly nine months and two weeks this prayer was said, and here she is, looking at two awesome creatures being breastfed by their mother.

"Is it her prayer that was answered or a sort of coincidence? Whatever, the main thing is that God had finally wiped Nneka's tears and salvaged her from leading unending sleepless nights.

"Thank God for an answered prayer," she said. Chizoba looked at her aunt's face; "the smile oozing out from there is capable of building laughter; what a joy of motherhood." As a little child, Chizoba's love for babies is overwhelming. Her mother, during one of the Christmas holidays, in fulfillment of her promise to her should she take the first position in her class, bought her a toy baby, which she had long desired. To her, that was indeed the best gift she had ever received from mankind. She would use her mom's wrapper and tie the baby on her back anywhere she went. Sometimes, she would bring the toy-baby out, and in a motherly position, acts as if she is breastfeeding Ifunanya – the name she gave her toy-baby. She and her friend Ada would most times save a little money and buy wool, which they would use to plait their toy babies.

"I can't wait to grow up, marry a good husband and have my own babies; preferably twins, a girl, and a boy," she told Nneka. "That's good, my dear, but you have more important things to focus on now that you have not bought the hen talk more of her laying and hatching the eggs, 'Nneka chuckled in reply. "Your ultimate ambition should be to become a successful woman, breaking the yoke of not being a housewife but a breadwinner of your future family too."

"Thanks for your words of admonishment and encouragement."

"You are welcome, dear."

"I'm really happy for you, mommy."

"Thank you, my daughter."

A lot of well-wishers were flooding the compound. This is not just a case of regular birth; rather, this is that of a couple that has consummated their marriage for good eighteen years without even a miscarriage. Miscarriages are not celebrated, but its occurrence at least is evidence that the woman in question is not barren; thus, there is still hope of another pregnancy.

As is the custom, provision is made for a powder or the traditional "Nzu," for those who had come to felicitate with them, to mark on their cheek, which is an indication that someone has been blessed with a child. The pattern of the marking of the powder or "Nzu" differs from the regular rubbing of powder on the face. On seeing such a person, the seer knows that a child has been born; he or she in addition immediately knows the gender as well and the number of children in the case of multiple births. A triple mark of the "Nzu" or powder on the right cheek signifies a male child, while a double mark on the left cheek shows that of a female child. In the case of a twin, it is marked on both sides of the cheeks with the appropriate markings. That of twins came to be after the abolishment of twin killings. Some after rubbing the powder drop a little token for the mother. This money is used for the child's upkeep, and it's donated out of one's goodwill and not by compulsion or any mandatory means.

Chizoba's joy doubled when she learned her mother would be coming for the "omugwo." As Nneka's only sister, coupled with the fact that their mother is now late, the onus falls on Adanma to go for her sister's "omugwo." Chizoba could not wait to set her eyes again on this woman whom she had dearly missed; if only she could fast-forward the hand of time. Nneka and her children were discharged two days later and were dropped home by Ukadike, her husband. A happy and lucky man he indeed is. At least he can now stand and talk freely and boldly in the "umunna" (Kindred) meetings without receiving mind-blowing insults from those stupid people that think all is well with them. He is very ready to lavish his wife with "nsala" soup and other edibles, which are required of her to consume in quantum within this postpartum period. He's now a proud father of two. If you think you are happier than Ukadike, show forth your face, let's behold!

After eight days, the boy child was circumcised, and both male and female were named amidst great party and jubilation. The boy was named Chukwudi, while the female counterpart was named Chinazaekpere.

* * *

"The saying that man proposes but God disposes has been made manifest.

A gigantic iroko tree has been uprooted by a mere wind!

Oh! How have the mighty fallen!

The ceremony of innocence is drowned

The blood-dimmed tide is loosened

The center has indeed broken into particles, and the falcon can no longer hear the falconer.

A gaze blank and pitiless as the sun has finally moved its slow thighs.

The darkness has beclouded the heavens

Even death itself is sober and claims accidental discharge in cover

Things have really fallen apart to the widest chagrin

A cry so intense that it pierces the ears of the deaf and seeks a passage from the dumb's mouth.

Two should have been taken to appease the land.

A lullaby will be soothing for this cause, but what's the essence if it lacks the sleeping ingredients in it.

Like a tasteless salt, it has been left for the feet to tread.

Oh! How have the mighty fallen!

A fierce fall has broken the camel's back.

It is said that the shooting of an owl shows a bad omen, but what happens when a committee of owls is shot?

Here lies dead the woman; a feed to mother-earth; the body that once breathed.

All in a lifeless sense, moping at the sky with closed eyes.

If only the sky could halt these wails which had formed to tear it apart like a whirlwind."

"Thank God it was just a dream," Chizoba muttered.

She couldn't really wait to behold her mother after such a long period of time away from home. She is going to tell her about life in the City and how good her new family has been to her. The urge to tell her about her mind-reader friend is something that has grown so strong and insurmountable within her. Is it possible she had a twin sister that she knows not about or is in any way related to royalty; if not, why does she bear the same surname with her Christabel, who claims Igwe Atikpa is her uncle? Maybe there are many things her mom had kept away from her for some reasons best known to her. But thank goodness she's coming today to provide an answer to all her worries.

The dream she had the previous night still looks fresh and so real to her. The fact that she consecutively had three nightmares in a single night is still something that seems necessarily strange to her.

"What could this actually mean?" she had said to nobody in particular. A spectator might think she's going nuts because it is only a mad man that can talk to an empty space. The look on her face is but that of a bitter-soul.

In the first dream, she had woken up very early in the morning, as usual, to do her morning functions to avoid being late for school. As she was washing the dishes that were used the previous day, the water she was using suddenly turned to blood. Giving out a loud shout, she had headed to her aunt's room to relate the happenings to her, only to get the most terrible shock of her life. She couldn't believe her eyes. The same Nneka that it took so long to hear the cry of a baby in her home was eating her two children and drinking their blood. On coming closer to have a clear view of what was happening, the figure that looked like her aunt suddenly turned into a dog and started advancing towards her. She tried running only to discover that her legs had become so heavy and transfixed to the ground. On catching up with her, the dog gave out a hysterical laugh and transformed into a crocodile. Immediately it opened its mouth wide to swallow her; she woke up panting heavily.

Not quite long, she slept the second time, and another nightmare surfaced, this time a more frightening one.

In the dream, Nneka and her husband had gone out with the children leaving her all alone in the house. She decided to take a nap. As she was sleeping, she heard a familiar voice calling her from outside; it was the voice of her mom. A voice she had so much missed for three years now. She immediately sprang on her feet and rushed towards the door. To her utter disbelief, no one was at the door. Suddenly, everywhere became dark, so dark that nothing at all could be seen. She felt a hand on her neck, followed by a thunderous slap. She passed out, only to regain herself in an uncompleted building with her hands and legs tied together. Nobody was in the room. On looking around, she saw candles of different colors placed in what seemed like an altar and a big mortar and pestle placed by the side. In a twinkle of an eye, Nneka and Ukadike entered in a procession-like manner with an unknown old man. The man performed some incantations on her and had her placed in the mortar. He handed the pestle over to Nneka and her husband, and they both started pounding her.

The third dream seemed so different and direct. She had come home from school to behold a large crowd crying in their compound. She asked what the matter was but got no reply. She tried going inside to keep her school bag and, on the way, met her mom. Overwhelmed with excitement, she tried to hug her but instead passed through her. Her mom just told her she was coming back and left. When she entered her room, a white casket was placed in the middle, and people were seeing the person inside of it one after the other. What baffled her the most was that she had never seen any of the faces before in her life. On peeping in the coffin, behold it was her mother lying inside.

"Thank God it was a dream."

She stood up from the bed, said her prayers, and proceeded to her usual morning chores. Fear of the unknown has indeed clouded her mind, but she will keep the dreams to herself till her mother comes.

Adanma is set to go to the City. For two weeks now, she has been preparing for this journey to give her sister a nice treat. She has gotten some foodstuffs within her reach, which she intends to bring to her. She took out time to prepare the "ugba" herself. Not only is Nneka so dear to her, being her only sister as well as brother is in itself an assurance to an inestimable love.

The demise of Ulaku, their mother, had automatically made her Nneka's mother being the first issue, and she has pledged within herself to take up the responsibility to her best ability. Adanma is in a very high spirit. The last time she visited her sister was when she was hospitalized, and now she's going for a good cause. The fact that Nneka has finally been salvaged from the association of barren-hood is a thing that gives her so much joy. It was on Saturday morning. Adanma had gone so early to the village park so as not to miss the only bus that conveyed people to the City. The bus only goes to the City twice daily, one in the early morning and the other late in the night. Adanma never loved traveling at night. The experience she got the day she engaged in one was not something she could forget in a hurry.

On that fateful day, she had come to park by 7:50 in the morning, only to notice that the God is good bus had long set out for its morning travel. Because of the urgency of her travel, she had no other choice than to wait till night travel, so she would be able to reach the City the following morning. On their way, their bus was laid siege by armed robbers who carted away with everything they had with them. She nearly collapsed when one of them pointed his gun at her. She didn't even know when she gave out the money she tied on the head of her wrapper. This time around, Adanma left at dawn to the village park. By exactly 8 o'clock, their bus zoomed off and entered the highway to the City amidst great hope. She really wants to see her daughter and give her that tight hug of a mother and give her the gifts she bought for her.

Everything on earth has its expiration date, so with the days of man, and where one's "Chi" fails him, there he dies, and that becomes his fate. Adanma had embarked on the journey of no return to the land of the ancestors.

The accident was so fatal that no survivor was recorded. The drunk driver had run into a fuel-loaded trailer, and an outburst of unquenchable fire took its course.

Halfway to the journey, the driver cleared so that people could stretch their backs and legs, and if possible, eat from the nearby restaurants. Osuofia had run into an old friend. After exchanging pleasantries, they went to a nearby bar to have a treat. Nothing is sweeter when one eats or drinks on all expenses paid. Being a wine glutton and a freeloader, Osuofia drank beyond his alcohol gauge. As a matter of necessity, he continued the journey, a careless and reckless decision that not only took his life in a most painful way but that of all on board the bus.

Chizoba fainted on hearing the news of her mother's death. The shocking news was so unbearable for her that she was in a coma for four good days. It took millions of words of consolation to get her back on track again.

"Mama, why now?"

She had always prayed for the day she would spoil her mother with goodies as an appreciation token for all her motherly love and care. Now her mom is gone even without saying goodbye. One thing about death is that it is inevitable, and the wish is not to die but to die a good death; one encountered when senility had set in.

Barely one week after her mother's funeral, had hell come seeking with its full force.

CHAPTER EIGHT

Oh let the wickedness of the wicked come to an end, but establish the just: for the righteous God tries the hearts and reins, though they pretend a just cause against me, yet God will judge their hypocrisy

— Psalm 7:9

Chizoba came to know misery after the death of her mother. As if in search of a better place to carry out their heinous plans, Nneka and her family moved out to a new place where they were not known. Why such an illicit act was being perpetrated on an innocent young girl was something that had defied reasonable explanations. The known fact was that Nneka's attitude to her niece continued depreciating immediately she had her own children and geared momentum of the highest level after the death of Adanma. At least there was no one left now that could question her actions towards the girl.

"Why is all this happening to me?"

"God, please come and take me too to where you have taken my mother to."

"I have been brought and abandoned in this wicked world with no one to speak for me."

The trauma of losing her virginity to her aunt's husband was too unbearable for her. All her plea couldn't stop the worthless man from raping her amidst her cry of pain. The case is already a frequent occurrence. She had been abused sexually by Ukadike to the point of reckless abandon. The worst part was when Nneka became aware of the sexual exploit, she did nothing, and instead, her actions suggested she endorsed it. She remembered how Nneka had treated her the day she complained to her after the first sexual abuse. She had hysterically laughed at her, with the saying that "it served her right." Later, she related to her husband that Chizoba had been making news of him.

"So, it implies I can't tell you to keep something a secret?" Ukadike said to Chizoba, his eyes red as blood. On seeing him in such a mood, she already knew that a lifetime beating would be the end product.

"I heard you have been going about the neighborhood telling them all sorts of rubbish about me," he said, ranting.

"Talk now before I kill you with my bare hands."

"I didn't say anything to any neighbor; I only told your wife about it considering the fact that she's now my mother," she struggled in reply.

"Oh! You told her, thinking she will kill me, right? Indeed, you are more than stupid for trying to paint me black in front of my wife. Don't you know that it's even a privilege that I'm making out with you? "

He pulled his belt and taught her a lesson she would never forget in her life and still had sex with her. She had become a chronic latecomer in school. Many of her teachers, including the principal, had beaten and warned her on so many occasions on her late coming attitude, coupled with the fact that she did sleep in class and the drastic drop in her academic performance. "If only they knew what she passed through every morning before being allowed to go to school. " The only person that was aware of her predicament was Christabel, but being a little girl of the same age with her, she practically had little or nothing to offer.

Her suffering took a different dimension when she was withdrawn from school. She had finished doing her daily morning routine. Looking at the time, it was still 9 o'clock; at least she's going one hour earlier today. On several occasions, she had been asked to go home for coming so late. Thank God for the school gateman that always took pity on her by allowing her in on a daily basis. She quickly rushed for her school bag, made for the door, and was stopped halfway by a call from her aunt.

"Bia, this girl, come back here."

"Where on earth do you think you are going with that bag? Can't you use your initiative for once and understand that your services are required more here? I think it's high time you stopped going to this useless school of yours. Training you in school makes no sense because you can't achieve anything good in life.

"Mommy, I'm already through with what you asked me to do, "she replied.

"So, I should start clapping for you for doing what you are expected to do? And point of correction, I can't be a mother to an evil child, so let this be the last time you address me as such again because I'm not your wretched dead mother, or do you want to kill me as you killed her?

Chizoba stood motionless, tears rolling down from her eyes. If only tears could change the hand of time. Here she is, being accused of the death of her mother. Had it been that she wasn't coming for the "omugwo," she wouldn't have died. She wishes the earth should just open its mouth and swallow her. Why is Nneka, of all people being this wicked; why inflicting both physical and emotional pain on her?

Nneka rose from where she was sitting, forcefully took her school bag from her, and had it incinerated. "From today henceforth, you're going to stop school. You are no way better than the people hawking in the streets because you are even eviler than them. You are a witch, and even the holy book made it clear that we should suffer, not your kind to live" Chizoba broke down in tears. All her aspirations of becoming somebody great in the nearest future had been shattered. The mirror of her dreams is now left in shambles. The only thing remaining that gives her joy and hope has now been taken away from her.

She couldn't understand why the only person she has left in the world had suddenly turned against her; a person her own mother lost her dear life trying to please. The imagination of what had come over the one good family she used to know had become so strong in her. Why should Nneka change now that God has finally blessed her with the fruit of the womb? The children she so much loved have now become a connecting point of her sorrow. Nneka and her husband would leave the little children with her at night and go inside their room to sleep or, on some occasions, go clubbing, leaving her to stay awake almost all through the night. In the morning, she would sweep the whole public compound, scrub the rooms in their apartment, cook for the family, fetch water, wash the clothes, and return to carry the babies after.

"What does a thirteen-year-old girl know about nursing a child? Talk more of when they are two?"

Nneka has now formed the habit of hanging out with different men. She would pour the breast milk into a bottle and hand it over to Chizoba to take care of the children before going out with any of her big fish. Ukadike, on the other hand, hardly stayed at home. What annoyed Chizoba the most was that she gets beaten even if she didn't do anything wrong. On one occasion, Nneka accused her of duping her husband and beat the hell out of her. What actually happened was that Chizoba was cooking, and the kerosene in the stove finished in the process. On realizing that there was no more kerosene in the container, she asked Ukadike for money so she could buy the kerosene and then finish with the cooking. Nneka later came back and gave her a hot beating with the accusation that there was kerosene in the house and that she just duped her husband in the pretense of buying kerosene.

The beating had now become a daily occurrence for her. Ukadike showing the magnanimity of his own wickedness, had bought three "koboko," with which she was always beaten. Neighbors do hear her daily cries, but one thing about living in the City is that people do mind their business. Nobody cares about his/her neighbor's actions as far as it is not affecting him or her in one way or the other. As graduation of her suffering, she was given a bowl and a bag of sachet water to hawk the streets any time her madam is around to take care of the children. Ukadike is a comfortably rich man and as such, subjecting her to such additional tedious work is nothing but sheer wickedness on their part. Her meals were reduced to once daily, and she was sure to face hell each day she couldn't finish up with the sales.

On one occasion, Chizoba was raped in the cause of doing her hawking business. The man had told her to come inside his house to collect money for the groundnut he bought. Unsuspecting, Chizoba immediately followed the man to his house. To her, the man was God sent. It was already evening, and she would soon be going home to face her punishment since she had up to fifteen cups of groundnut still remaining. The man had opted to buy the whole groundnut. When it was time to pay, the man pretended to have forgotten his wallet in his house, which was just a stone throw away. Chizoba couldn't miss this somewhat excellent opportunity; she followed the man to his house, happy that she was going to escape being beaten.

When they reached the house, Chizoba waited outside while the man entered to get the money. The man came out, standing on the door with the money in his hands. While pretending to be on a call, he motioned to Chizoba to come and collect her money. Poor Chizoba didn't know she was entering a trap. On reaching out, the man held her by the hand and quickly drew her inside and locked the door. Two other men were already in wait with marijuana in their hands and assorted hot drinks on the table. Placed on the table was also a gun. Chizoba tried shouting but kept her cool on sighting the gun. She was so frightened inside of her and was wondering what they wanted from her.

Chizoba knew it was going to be yet another sad incidence following the order that came afterward. She was told to pull off her clothes. On hearing the order, Chizoba had no choice but to comply because the fear of the gun they say is the beginning of wisdom. Also, there was nothing she could do to overpower three men. Her fear heightened when one of the men opened the gun and inserted some cartridges. She knows that the only way she can go out from there in good health is for her to give her maximum compliance. Chizoba was mercilessly raped for up to two hours by the three men gang and was later pushed out of the house. At least, they were kind enough to give her the money she had come to collect; if not, what on earth would she tell her madam happened to the groundnut and also the money.

On reaching home, she decided to keep the unfortunate incident to herself because Nneka and her husband were no different and also had, in one way, molested her sexually. At her age, she had been made to undergo four abortions courtesy of Ukadike.

CHAPTER NINE

Chizoba makes sales by carrying goods, traveling about 12-13 hours daily to wherever she can find a buyer. Countless times, she treks a very long distance or wanders about selling goods she carries on her head. We know that children by nature suffer fatigue easily. As hawking poses long hours of strenuous trekking (heavy loads on the head), the fatigue increases the demand for rest which may not be satisfied. Consequently, the fatigue leads to chances for accidents and stress-related diseases. Daily, these children put themselves into trouble. There are incidents where child hawkers who chase moving cars and cluster near traffic jams are knocked down by other moving vehicles, leading to injuries, bone fracture and amputation, maiming, and death. Due to long hours of wandering about and lack of time to rest and eat, Chizoba experienced physical exertion, malnutrition, and premature aging.

On several occasions, she was attacked by mad people, rapists, ritualists, and child traffickers as she moved about to sell her groundnut. Nneka has denied Chizoba some days' meals while she receives thorough beatings and is chased out of the house in the night as punishment for lost items. This attitude has exposed her to emotional health problems, sexual molestation with its sexually transmitted infections, kidnapping, trafficking, injuries, body pain, and malnutrition.

Chizoba started hawking groundnut for Nneka and became a truant, missing lessons, totally absent in the class, which made her perform low academically. She doesn't have time and energy for the take-home assignments and home studies as she always goes home late in the night and is too tired to do any academic work.

Chizoba and other street hawkers have become prime targets for robbery and assault because they fear contacting the authorities. Their perpetrators prey on their vulnerability because they know they can go scot-free.

A few weeks ago, two young men approached Antonio on Bright Street and 10th Avenue and fired five gunshots in his direction, Chizoba told Nneka, but she cared less to her story. Antonio was able to shield himself with his truck for protection. The bullet strikes remain on the truck and are a reminder that he could have lost his life that day for the 100 naira that he had in his pocket. Antonio threw himself behind his truck and stayed there for a while. He couldn't move until someone came up to him moments later to see if he was OK.

Our fear, Chizoba said, has now gone to a new level due to the recent death of Kelvin, another Bright Street vendor who sold snacks in his neighborhood from a truck he would push, who was gunned down on April 20. He was shot at about 9.30 p.m. Armed robberies are not their only obstacles; they are often bullied by gangsters, cultists, and teens in the neighborhood. Sometimes they come and throw their goods on the ground, laugh, and leave. Another one is that City officials will throw away their products for lacking a street-hawking license. They don't defend themselves because they genuinely don't want any trouble. They don't want to fight; they just want to work. When such an incident happens, some street hawkers do contact authorities, but by the time police arrive, the robbers are long gone, and it is too late.

Here's another ordeal of a street hawker in the hands of arm robbers. Alien Avenue is trying to come to grips with the murder of a beloved street vendor who they say took care of everybody who crossed his path. "He got along with everybody, and everybody knew him," said George, whose father was shot and killed on Tuesday night in the neighborhood where he was so well known for the snacks he would sell from his truck. They killed him to steal the little money he had on him.

Alexander the deceased always walked his grandchildren to school every morning when George would go to work. George was worried about how his kids would take the news of the demise of their grandfather. He helped him a lot with his kids. He said, "Now they're going to be walking to school alone," as people of all ages poured into their house to sympathize with their family. Alexander was gunned down on Friday while he was selling his snacks. He was shot as he was trying to flee from two men who confronted him. A day after the shooting, his relatives and friends mourned together in his home. His house was filled and quiet, but his wife Esther wept uncontrollably, knowing she would never see her husband. The killing left neighbors shaken as well.

Mary, an eyewitness, said she called the police after Friday's shooting. She was in her bedroom when her son rushed up to her. She thought he was going to ask her for fifty naira to buy a snack from Alexander. "He said to her, 'Mommy, someone is pointing a gun at the man,' " Kingsley said. "He was here every day. He was a very nice, respectful man." Children in the neighborhood told stories about how Alexander gave them a snack with a promise to pay him back if they didn't have money. Sometimes he would just give it to them for free, they said. Alexander's wife wanted to speak to Kingsley on Saturday morning because he was the last person to see him alive. "How much money does he have on him? He lost his life because of a fifty naira note," Kingsley said. George said his father had always wanted to go back to the village to take care of their house. Their family is facing a decision whether to bury him in the City or bury him in his native home.

Sadly, Chizoba was robbed and pistol-whipped one day in the street while hawking her groundnut. Two men who appeared to be in their 30s demanded money from her, she refused, and the robbers showed her a gun which they now used to pistol-whip her; she sustained a small cut on the back of her head. The robbers stole about one thousand five hundred naira from her pocket and fired a shot into the ground. That's when 13-year-old Rosas got involved. The incident occurred in the street right in front of her house. She said she and her brother initially thought the shot was a firework, but then they went outside to see Chizoba on the ground and two men running away. "I need help; I'm bleeding from my back," Chizoba said. "And that's when Rosas and her mom went outside, and they called the police, and that's when the robbers ran away." Cary, who lives only a few doors away, said she recognized the street hawker as someone who "comes up and down the street almost every day" and said she's surprised that this type of incident happened in what she called a "quiet" neighborhood. "It's so surreal," she said. "You hear this on the news and think it's not going to happen in your neighborhood, and then it does, so I guess we have to be more cautious." Rosas said the incident made her nervous since it involved a gun. "It's scary because if I go to the bus stop, what if someone does that?" she said. "I might need someone here to watch me go to the bus stop. It's scary." Chizoba was treated at the scene for minor injuries.

Afterward, one day two men were chasing after a vendor, pushing him to the ground and punching and kicking him, then robbing him. When bystanders tried to help, one of the suspects waved a gun at them. The suspect also used the gun to strike the vendor, and they got away with cash and a cell phone. The two suspects fled the scene in a Mercedes-Benz coupe. The incident happened on Monday around 4:20 p.m. in Federal Housing Avenue. The suspects were about 20 to 25 years old and 5 feet 6 inches tall. One of them was dressed in a black hoodie and khaki trousers, and the other was dressed in a grey sweater and light blue pants. Medlin stopped his push truck downtown and reached inside for a paleta. Within seconds, he was knocked unconscious. When the 58-year-old street hawker opened his eyes, he was on the ground and surrounded by people. His head "hurt a lot," and his wallet was gone. Medlin, who was robbed on Monday, is among several street vendors who have been beaten and robbed in recent months in the neighborhood.

"They didn't say anything. They just hit me and knocked me out," Medlin said. Medlin said he had just started walking through the streets of Housing Estate with his truck on Monday when a man and a woman approached him, asking him for an ice pop. Medlin reached inside the push truck seconds before one of them punched him and knocked him to the ground. The two robbers (a man and woman) brutally robbed the ice cream man. The robbers searched Medlin before fleeing in a black Toyota Avalon. The police are yet to arrest the suspects. Medlin has no family in Onitsha and spent nearly three days in the hospital for a head injury. He said he still feels disoriented, suffers constant pain in his head, and cannot walk by himself.

An activist by the name of Zavion, after hearing multiple reports of street hawkers being attacked, became fed up after a 68-year-old ice cream man died earlier in the month after he was shot while being robbed in Main Market. "From that moment, I kind of lost it," He said. "I've had enough, you know, because it's my raza (people) ... (I thought) if I have a voice, I got to speak out." Zavion, a community activist, started a campaign to raise funds to buy pepper spray for all street hawkers in the city of Onitsha and the environs who work by themselves. He delivered the first pepper spray kit to a few hawkers because he wanted to put up some form of protection so that they can have a chance to run. "It's not illegal to carry pepper spray, and you can use it in self-defense," he said."

Interestingly, within a few weeks, he and other volunteers had met with about 60 street hawkers, giving them pepper spray kits and teaching them how to use them. "When they walk through our streets, they should feel secure, and they should feel protected," he said. Street hawkers can use pepper spray to protect themselves if they are getting assaulted; they have every right to protect themselves. They need to feel safe again.

CHAPTER TEN

God has never failed and cannot fail now. "Those who put their trust in God shall mount on wings like eagles; they shall walk and not grow weary; they shall run and not faint."

It was on a Saturday morning, Chizoba finally got done with the operose & arduous house chores, "This girl must have possessed some sort of Herculean powers of the Hercules in her past life or something." If there is a better adjective to qualify how strong Chizoba is and how high-spirited she is, I would prefer "virile." She is a girl who's got these iron-like nerves and determination, so intriguing mostly in her beard's own performance in the exhibition of the body grueling house chores.

Having a strong will to survive and not minding the trials and hardship of life, which more importantly is the major thing that keeps one going in life; "determination and willingness to live." She picks up her hawking basket as she sets for the day's hawking, and meanwhile, her aunty changes the item she sells indecisively as the poor girl was always left with no choice nor option.

It happened that she has diverted to hawking of gala and chilled drinks which in most African countries, it is commonly seen to be boys who do this type of risky hawking because this requires running on the road and chasing after moving vehicles sometimes and if lucky enough, they get to sell in traffic jams.

"I know we would be wondering if Nneka (Chizoba's aunt) still got some conscience left as a human. Crazily as it may sound, but the honest truth is that when life decides to dehumanize one and to try to make it a hell on earth for one, it tends to make someone a devil in disguise just to kill down that thing that has been deposited in you. I would say Nneka's conscience was already far gone as she turned the devil's incarnate just to make life difficult and hell for Chizoba."

In the contemporary society we exist in today, those who are less privileged get to be easily trampled on as they claimed they have no say in the society, which makes them face negative societal vices.

Chizoba got to where she sells her gala and immediately joined her fellow hawkers in the line of business. She was nicknamed a "tomboy." This was as a result of the tomboyish nature of her business. Sometimes she was mocked and intimidated, but that was not enough reason to yield to the sluttish and slatternly advice of some of the promiscuous girls who already accepted their bad fate in a negative and indecent way. She possessed her late mother's virtue and pride. She always believed she was different and wonderfully created to oblige and compromise to such a lifestyle.

The road was lousy as usual, car beeps everywhere, and some rough drivers and commercial drivers try to find and manipulate their way to escape from the traffic jam which had turned as usual. One must be careful even in such situations as they tend to be crazy drivers. Chizoba was attending to a lady in a Lexus 350. She asked Chizoba to bring a chilled Coca-Cola drink with two galas. Chizoba being very swift, quickly attended to her. She collected her money, and while crossing to answer someone else and probably look for more customers because she won't dare come home with remnants of her sales, she did not foresee the crazy driver who had followed the wrong lane. Before Chizoba could know it, she was already knocked down by the bus. The driver knowing the consequences of his action, immediately fled, probably he thought the girl was dead. Immediately people gathered, and as bad as society has turned, people wouldn't rush a dying patient immediately to the hospital but rather start taking pictures immediately just to upload on social media rather than saving a life first.

Chizoba was in a pool of her blood as she was unconscious. Luckily, there was a Good Samaritan who saw the scene and immediately alighted from his car, and he happened to be a doctor. He picked her up with the help of some people. He took her to the hospital for immediate treatment. Luckily as we may have it, Chizoba only broke her leg and got some scratches on the face. The doctor, which is very rare to find today, proceeded with the treatment without waiting for the little girl's parents or guardian. She was given all medical attention and care, and he did all his best to ensure she was saved.

Waking up, Chizoba felt excruciating pains all over her body. She was still trying to recall what transpired. Then she remembered she had been hit by a hit-and-run driver. Not quite long, the doctor approached her, though not knowing who he was, she greeted politely, and the doctor responded to her.

Chizoba, who was already in tears, asked the doctor for her basket of gala and money. The doctor was surprised at how she was able to ask for those irrelevant stuff amidst the pain, making the doctor feel pity for the young girl. He already scrutinized and knew the girl's situation and immediately calmed her down by telling her they are safe. Indeed, Chizoba was really pathetic. He sighed and said to his mind, "Only if my wife would give in to adoption or bring someone home." The doctor was married to a boss lady who is so bossy and most times stubborn and had a say in the family decision. The doctor told her to relax and provided her with the necessary things she needed. One of the nurses later explained to Chizoba that the doctor was the one who saved her life; indeed, he was her life savior. Chizoba couldn't stop thanking and appreciating the doctor from the depth of her heart. Nneka, on the other hand, wasn't even bothered by the whereabouts of the young child she sent hawking. She never cared if she was devoured by an animal or kidnapped or anything; all she cared about was her children.

The following day after the doctor had waited enough, he asked Chizoba about her parents, which she later explained that they were late. She only stays with her aunt and uncle. The doctor asked her if there was a way she could contact them, and Chizoba remembered a time she personally had to memorize her Aunt's phone digit. She called out the number, and the doctor dialed it.

Nneka's phone rang, and she picked up. The doctor asked for her identity, to which she responded. He told her about the situation on the ground and gave her the direction and location of the hospital where Chizoba was hospitalized. Nneka knowing the consequences and detriment of a Child's ill-treatment in human rights, quickly faked the reaction one would get from a caring and loving mother on the phone.

She hissed after the call, took her time to prepare before she left for the hospital. On getting there and as usual, Chizoba was expecting her usual reaction, but her heart almost fell out from her mouth when Nneka immediately hugged her and started shedding crocodile tears. Chizoba knowing fully well what was going on, got heartbroken not because Nneka hugged her but because it had been a while she got hugged and loved by someone, even if it was faked. Indeed, the scene was as touchy as it may seem to people who don't know what was going on. Nneka paid the remaining bills and decided to take Chizoba home. Immediately they left the hospital; she left Chizoba alone immediately to walk on her own.

"Get away from me, you stinking bitch, a curse in disguise. I see they have sent you to drain the savings we have, right?" she asked rhetorically amidst loud screaming.

Chizoba was already becoming conversant with her attitudes and devilish behaviors that she already made up her mind to always expect the worst from her aunt. Chizoba managed to walk with the crutches given to her to assist her in walking as a result of her broken leg. She entered the car, and they drove home. "Chizoba would prefer the hospital rather than that hell of a house if she was given a chance."

This was a sort of blessing in disguise as she got a break from hawking under the hot weather, though that didn't stop her from performing other house chores and tasks, and enduring the unnecessary and wicked scolding attached to it.

"Man is supreme lord and master
Of his own ruin and disaster,
Controls his fate, but nothing less
In ordering his own happiness:
For all his care and providence
Is too feeble a defense
To render it secure and certain
Against the injuries of Fortune;
And oft, in spite of all his wit,
Is lost by one unlucky hit,
And ruined with a circumstance,
And mere punctilio of a chance."

A few months later, Chizoba was getting better, and her bones were healing. If it were to be some people, they would have worn a pretense face and claimed not to be better to avoid the jezebel's, another mind-blowing line of action. But it was not the case in Chizoba. When her aunt found out immediately that she was better, at least now she could walk without the aid of crutches though she still leaps, she immediately told her to resume work immediately. She told her she was of no help at home even though Chizoba would still bathe, cook, wash, scrub and feed her children even when she had a broken leg. But Nneka counted them all as useless. All she cared about was money. She had decided to turn her into a money-making machine and also torment her life.

If not for reasons best known to Nneka, which she guarded jealously, she would have asked Chizoba to go into prostitution, and that would fetch her enough money, but thank goodness she didn't. After some months and a long break, Chizoba returned to her hawking lifestyle. Looking entirely new and tiring, she still had to get used to it again.

This time around, her predicament was worse than the former. She got up in the morning and, as usual, said her morning prayer secretly because she had been warned heinously never to pray again in that house as it was regarded as useless. So, she does this secretly because she believed her help would only come from God, the author, and the finisher of one's fate. She did her usual chores and left for hawking. She got all ready and left. Accepting her fate but still hopes for a change. She missed some of her hawking mates because she got to smile sometimes during her interactions with them. One's got to live. Some people asked about her well-being, one thing is for sure, and which is people's likeness towards her and a lot of people admired her high spiritedness, while some admired her hard work and her decency in all ramifications.

Everything became normal again except for the fact that she still leaps while walking, but still, it didn't stop her from running. It happened that she finished up her sales very early that very day and she was joyous, but as fate may have it, she never knew the worst was about to happen. She was going home happily in other to make a return when a white bus crooked and stopped in front of her. Immediately she sensed this was a bad sign as her instinct already told her that the way the bus stopped was very dangerous. Then as she was about to pick to her heels, she was outrun. Her legs couldn't allow her to run. Immediately she was held strongly and firmly by two robust men who bounded her into the bus, and like no single soul was on the scene that moment, they drove off to only God knows where. Chizoba was snuffed with drugs as she slept off in other for them to be able to cross some police checkpoints. They drove for a long distance and entered a bush path.

They arrived at an uncompleted building which was probably their hideout. They came down and brought down Chizoba from the bus and tied her down. When Chizoba woke up, she saw herself amidst other young girls who were all tied and numbered on the forehead. Anything stronger than fear gripped her immediately, and she knew she was helpless at seeing the size of the hefty men standing there. She couldn't scream as she already knows what would precede the action. She tried assimilating the situation on ground as she prays earnestly in her mind for help from God. She is a strong believer in Christ. She said all sorts of prayers in her heart, and it was then she overheard one of the men answering a call, but before then, she was already number 15.

These men (kidnappers) do this as a business. They kidnap young girls as they sell them to the ritualist and some politicians who use them for either money rituals or sex machines and slaves. Chizoba eavesdropped on the call, and more fear gripped her. "Smally calm down, you are too fine, and you will definitely make a good pay but don't worry, you won't fall under the ritualist but probably the sex slave because you look like the type that would be good on bed ooo, fine girl," one of the kidnappers said to Chizoba. Chizoba was in tears already as she wasn't able to predict her fate anymore. "What wrong have I committed on this earth? Who has laid a curse on me? Why is my own life so brutal and hard?" All these questions crossed her mind as she broke down in tears. Then it was then she remembered a popular verse she hears in the Bible in the nearby church beside her house. She secretly fellowshipped with them from their apartment.

She prayed a prayer in Psalm 121, which says:

"I will lift up my eyes to the hills—
From whence comes my help?
My help *comes* from the Lord,
Who made heaven and earth.
He will not allow your foot to be moved;
He who keeps you will not slumber.
Behold, He who keeps Israel
Shall neither slumber nor sleep.

The Lord *is* your keeper;
The Lord *is* your shade at your right hand.
The sun shall not strike you by day,
Nor the moon by night.

The Lord shall preserve you from all evil;
He shall preserve your soul.
The Lord shall preserve your going out and your coming in
From this time forth, and even forevermore."

She remembered she had a God who never slumbers nor sleeps and immediately some sort of strength from above which would be considered divine endowed and empowered her. She had faith she won't die.

These men sometimes go to sleep with some of the girls before selling them off while they keep some in case a customer requires a virgin which they consider more expensive. A call came in, and it happened that a buyer was ready to buy one of them, and that was when she heard them telling the buyer that they got a new fresh one and she looked pretty and definitely going to be good for a sex slave.

There was a noise in the bush, and this brought about distraction. They felt it was some kind of people who had located them. So, they brought out their guns to look for what it could be and, if possible, engage in combat. Chizoba quickly fought really hard to loosen herself. This she had been trying ever since she was tied but to no avail, but immediately they left her sight, all of a sudden she loosened herself, and to her greatest surprise, she was freed. She looked at the girls and wanted to help but knowing it would consume more time and the kidnappers would get back immediately. She decided to flee and instead get help and a rescue team for the other girls.

Nneka being a jezebel, wasn't even bothered about Chizoba's whereabouts. She concluded she must have had another accident, and she wasn't ready to spend a dime on her again.

Chizoba ran as her legs could take her, and like she was divinely empowered because with human capabilities, she was not supposed to be able to run so fast; after all, she had a problem with her leg, but as God may have it, she escaped it. While she was running, she started singing, "I have a God who never fails, I have a God who never fails, I have a God who never fails, who never fails, who never fails, Forevermore."

Getting closer to where the sound was heard, they happened to see a dead dog lying on the ground. Nobody could explain what transpired, but they were relieved it wasn't what they thought, and immediately they retreated to the camp. On getting there, they found out the new girl was nowhere to be found. Out of rage and fury, the boss ordered two of the boys to run after her immediately and kill her if possible because they know they would be endangered if she got to escape.

Immediately they ran after Chizoba like a flash but not knowing she had long gone. Chizoba ran tirelessly till she got to an express road where she got a bike and told the driver to take her to the nearest police station. Luckily, she met a good person because whoever saw the way she was panting and gasping for breath would definitely know something serious was wrong, and a lot of people wouldn't even stop to carry her while some would use that as an advantage. But she was lucky enough to meet a God sent.

By the time she got to the police station, she had narrated the whole story as she was told to make a statement first. Later, the D.P.O ordered a rescue team to go get the remaining girls, but only God knew if it was successful or not.

That was how Chizoba got delivered from the hands of kidnappers. When her aunt was notified of the situation, she again faked everything. Nneka is indeed a green snake in green grass, and she would make a good actress. She said to the police that she has been searching for her niece and had even made a statement already in the police station.

* * *

Chizoba experienced the worst form of inhumanity of man to his fellow man the very day Chukwudi fell from her hands. The day was very hectic for her. After going to bed around 2 am, she still had to wake up by 5 o'clock in the morning to accomplish her morning routine. She had to bathe the children, sweep the compound, and mop the floor and get the breakfast ready. Afterward, she went to the market to buy the items with which to cook "oha soup" for lunch. After cooking the soup, she cooked the groundnut, which she is supposed to hawk for the day, and set off to the market. During the afternoon, she had to come home to make "eba" for lunch, set the food on the dining table, informed her madam, and went back to the market to continue her sales. Left with no choice, she had come to love the hawking business, knowing so well that that's what the future holds for her and nothing better.

When she returned in the evening, she received her usual beating because she couldn't finish the heap of groundnuts her madam had sent her to sell. After crying for a while, she wiped her eyes, bathed the babies, and entered the kitchen to make food for the night, knowing fully well that failure to do so will attract even heavier punishments. Chizoba finished with the cooking around 8 pm and then had her first food for the day. Barely had she finished eating did Nneka call out to her to come and carry the children, so she could go to sleep.

"I'm coming, Madam; let me quickly rush and wash the dishes," she responded. Nneka had instructed her to always address her as her madam since she's nothing less than a maid to her. What some people fail to understand in this life is the fact that being nice to people you live with is of the utmost essence, for ninety-five percent of your life dwells with them, and they both variably and invariably have the keys to it. Making them happy is not only advisable, but a matter of necessity because overstretching their anger can earn you an automatic death warrant, thereby getting you closer to the world beyond.

"I don't know why you are so lazy," Nneka barked at her.

"Be fast with whatever you are doing and come and take care of these children so I can go and catch some sleep."

"Alright, Madam, please don't be so annoyed."

Like the flash of light, she quickly dashed to the kitchen, gathered the whole dirty plates, and started washing. As a bid to make things more difficult for her, Nneka and her husband usually eat with up to four plates each, and they will always make sure they soil the whole plates. She had warned Chizoba not to wash dishes immediately when they had finished eating so that the particles of the food would first stick hard on the dishes, making it difficult to wash. One might be wondering the kind of evil spirit that had taken control of Nneka's mind, for this was the same woman that took Chizoba as the apple of her eyes some years back and never failed to lavish her with good stuff when she had not given birth to her own children.

She could recall the very day she invited the police over to arrest their neighbor's son just because he tried beating her. She spent money to make sure the boy stayed up to a week in the police custody so that next time he won't have the audacity, the temerity, the alacrity, and the effrontery to talk to her talk more of pointing his filthy fingers at her. After washing the dishes, she quickly took her bath and rushed and carried the little innocent children.

"Make sure you keep an eye on them, especially on Chinaza because she's not feeling so fine." Nneka handed her over the bottled breast milk as usual and retired for the day. Both babies were crying; she tied Chinaza on her back and carried Chukwudi in her hands, and had to walk the whole room singing different lullabies to lure them to sleep since they keep crying anytime she tries sitting down. "Poor innocent children, if only they knew she had a very busy day and needed rest," she said to herself, having pity on them.

When it was already three o'clock in the morning, she couldn't hold on any longer. Nothing is so conscious of being cheated like nature. Nature would rather cheat you instead of the otherwise. As she was sitting down on the sofa, sleep took control of her, and in the process, Chukwudi, in a playful mood, slipped out of her hands. The devil surely has a way of his doings. Nneka did not see any other time to check on her children but now. The fall happened almost simultaneously with her stepping into the parlor. Witnessing the happening, she gave out a loud shout which not only woke Chizoba but placed her immediately on her feet. Nneka left her with a strong star sparkling slap and rushed over to her son. She ran an inspection, and miraculously nothing happened to him. The fact that the baby didn't give out a cry is more than mysterious; maybe God had sent His angels to take charge of him lest he strikes his feet on the ground as was promised Jesus by the biblical Satan; whatever. The most important thing is that nothing happened to the young Chukwudi.

It took up to ten minutes before Chizoba recovered from the mesmerizing effect of the slap. Nneka untied the baby on Chizoba's back and carried her children to her husband's room. When it was 8 o'clock in the morning, both Nneka and her husband stormed Chizoba's room with all that could better be termed the weapons of mass destruction. They stripped her stark naked and each armed with a "koboko," started showcasing their expertise. After beating her to their satisfaction, they decided to upgrade terror by leaving an indelible mark of their wickedness on the unlucky child.

The couple plugged and had the electric iron heated; they laid Chizoba on the floor and started pressing her back with the iron in a cloth-like manner. Her agony rented the air that even the devil and malicious demons had to come closer to learn work from this heartless couple, a cry that is capable of incurring God's wrath on the whole world. One could imagine how painful it can be when one's hand mistakenly kisses the blade of a heated iron while ironing. Here somebody's daughter is being made to pass through the agony of having the iron smear her whole back. Still not yet satisfied by their demoralizing actions, Nneka headed straight to the kitchen in search of another instrument of pain.

"Who knows whether the intention was just to punish her or to send her six feet below the earth?" Nneka pounded a handful of pepper and came back to the room with it. As if she intended blinding her or maybe just to prevent her from knowing their next line of action, she rubbed some of the paper in her eyes.

"Just imagine this kind of devilish attitude." Ukadike helped to spread her legs while Nneka did the main work. She started inserting the remaining pepper into Chizoba's private part. When they had exhausted their strength, they tied her hands and legs and locked her up inside the room, leaving her in so much pain. Nneka and her husband prepared and took their children to the hospital to make sure nothing happened to both of them. Poor Chizoba had already lost her voice to cry. The sonorousness of her voice had now turned to a lamb-like bleat.

"Death, why not come and take me?" she said, full of anguish.

Which one should she concentrate on; is it the pepper burn in her eyes or the one seriously burning her private part, or is it that of the iron or the injuries inflicted on her from the beatings? She is indeed BURIED IN THE DARK room and left to die.

CHAPTER ELEVEN

And we know that all things work together for good to those that love God, to those who are called according to His purpose. For whom He did foreknow, He also did predestinate to be conformed to the image of His Son, that he might be the firstborn amongst many brethren. Moreover, whom he did predestinate, them he also called, and whom He called, them he also justified, them He also glorified

—Romans 8: 28-30

The doctor and the nurses had been doing everything possible within their ambiance to make sure she survives. She had been given so many drips and injections to lessen the overall body pain and the burning effect of the pepper inside of her. Her current state is one capable of arousing pity from anybody, even the devil himself. She had passed out and has been in a coma for two days now. What gives people more concern is the fact that her eyes in which pepper was smeared have been closed since then. Practically, she had gone blind.

"Had it not been for the timely rescue, the young girl would have died, but of whether she is going to see again, I cannot tell; though there is still hope, that would be a case of a miracle."

The above was the exact wordings of the doctor when Mr. Livinus asked about the condition of the girl. Heavens will never rest for the man that had carried Chizoba to the hospital. Mr. Okwonkwo Livinus, or the Ironman as he has been nicknamed, is a poor mower that was employed to always cut the grasses in the Big Brothers Estate, which happened to be the place Ukadike and his family lives, which is nearly the largest in the City. Despite having lived in the City for more than good twenty-five years, and coupled with the fact that he works in a high-paying company, Ukadike cannot boast of a single block talk more of owning land or building in the village. He is such an Epicurean discipline that all his earnings are given out for enjoyment. His major hobbies include smoking, drinking, partying, and womanizing. The girls really love him because he is indeed a philanthropist when it comes to giving girls money. He is well known in almost all the brothels in the City.

Livinus, as his work entailed, had gone in the early hours of the day to cut grasses in the estate as usual. He is such a dedicated fellow that he does the menial job with all his heart. On this particular day, he was humming and mowing the grasses when suddenly, he was startled by the shout emanating from one of the buildings.

"Which building could this cry be coming from?" he was asking nobody in particular. He had wondered what might have been the cause of the loud cry. He continued doing his work but couldn't hold longer when the wailing had failed to subside. He began his trace and discovered it was coming from the eleventh building, which belonged to Mr. Ukadike. Nearly everyone in the estate knows of Ukadike and the wife's ill-mannered attitude towards Chizoba.

"What has this innocent young girl done to these people again? The fact alone that they allow her to hawk the streets is already a clear pointer to the incommensurate heartlessness.

Big Brother Estate is among the most expensive estates in the City, and no man considered average can cope with the exorbitant house rent. Prominent among the inhabitants are senior advocates, military Generals, Medical Doctors, Professors, Senators, big businessmen, and Ministers. By standard, all the people living in the estate are rich. Ukadike is a rich man, and so was no exception. People had expressed their uttermost shock when they discovered the young groundnut seller lived in the estate too. Knowing that the little girl no longer goes to school but has been made to hawk the streets gave some of them grieved hearts. Some even had the intention of helping her but paused halfway when they found out the kind of man Ukadike was. Ukadike was already notorious as one who always likes trouble. Practically, helping the little Chizoba is no way their business; they didn't know her before, neither do they know her village or any of her siblings, so intervening in such affair shouldn't be their headache, even though it pained most of them seeing the poor girl being maltreated. At least if they had known any of her relatives, they would have related to them the hell the little girl was passing through and would have even assisted in getting her evacuated.

After what had happened to Silas, most of the neighbors had decided to wash their hands and stay away from anything that had to do with Ukadike or anybody coming from his family. Ukadike is indeed one that loves trouble a whole lot. His likeness for court cases is unimaginable. He can spend the last money in his pocket just to perpetuate a case. Silas, out of his benevolence, had decided to help Chizoba the very day she was not allowed inside the house. Chizoba had gone to make her normal sales. On her way back home, rejoicing that she was able to get everything sold off, a group of young boys had boycotted her and made away with all the money she had with her, inclusive of the money she was to use in procuring some foodstuffs for the evening meal. Chizoba cried all through, and no help was coming forth. When she reached the house and narrated what had happened to her madam, as usual, she showcased her expertise. Chizoba was so terribly beaten into a bad shape for a thing that could happen to anybody. She was sent out of the house to go in search of the money despite the fact that it was raining heavily.

Silas was returning very late in the night in his car and saw a girl lying both helplessly and hopelessly in front of the estate gate amidst the heavy rain. He drew his car to a halt, alighted, and went closer to know if the girl was dead or something of such. He was blown by shock when he discovered that it was Chizoba. He woke her up and carried her to his house.

In his house, the wife helped her with water to bathe and served her good food. It was when Chizoba had finished eating that she was able to muster the energy to talk.

"What happened to you?" Silas asked.

Little Chizoba narrated her whole ordeal to Silas and his wife, who gave her audience. She told them of how she was robbed in the market after making her sales by some unknown and unscrupulous hoodlums. Of how she narrated the whole incident to her madam and was terribly beaten for a thing she had no control over and how her night food, which was the only food she was allowed to eat for the day, was denied her and how she was sent out in the rain, never to come back to the house without the money.

Silas's family had pity on the girl after listening to her narration and decided to help the young girl. They couldn't just understand how somebody created by God would be treating a fellow being like loads of trash just because she's not their daughter.

"How are you related to them?" Silas's wife asked.

"Ukadike's wife is my mother's only sister," she replied.

"My mother begged her to take me along to the City to lessen her financial burden owing to the death of my father."

"Where is your mother now and your village too?" Silas chipped in.

"My mother is now late."

"She died on her way to the City to take the "omugwo" responsibility for my madam since their mother had died and both of them were the only ones left." On hearing the story, tears of sorrow started rolling down the wife's cheeks. "What on earth can make somebody wicked over her sister's daughter." "So, the only way your aunty could pay your mother for sacrificing her life for her pleasure is to be treating her daughter like an animal?"

They decided to have her stay in their house. The following morning, Ukadike and his wife never cared to know about Chizoba's whereabouts. They continued their normal living as if to say nothing had happened. It was after three days that Nneka was passing by and beheld Chizoba in Silas's quarters. In the night, she narrated what she saw in the afternoon to her husband, and both partners in crime didn't waste time to devise their next line of action.

The early morning of the following day, Ukadike stormed Silas's compound in the company of some policemen and had him arrested. Without wasting time, he immediately sued the case to court. The allegations he levied against Silas were that of kidnapping and keeping his daughter against her own will. The case lingered for months, and save the fact that Silas is well connected, he would have languished in jail because the case of kidnapping is a serious issue that might even attract a death warrant. It was after this ugly incident that people decided in a Pilate-like manner to wash their hands off anything that had to do with Ukadike or his family. On reaching Ukadike's compound, Livinus had remembered what had happened to Silas and decided to retrace his steps. He knows Silas was able to get out of the whole mess because he was a wealthy and connected fellow, but what would be his own case. He can't always boast of daily three-square meal talk more of having extra to pursue a case.

"Livinus, you better mind yourself," he had told himself.

He went back to continue with his work. It was later when he saw Ukadike and his wife drive off in their car, and when he could not hear the cries again that he decided to check to know what had transpired, knowing fully well that she was not allowed to enter their car.

On reaching the house, he discovered that the door was locked from outside.

"Is it possible that she went with them, or was she locked inside?

He had decided to go back to his work when something caught his gaze. One of the windows was half-closed. Livinus went closer to have a peep through the window and, behold what his eyes saw, could make a heavily pregnant woman have an instant miscarriage. There lies Chizoba writhing in severe pain. The young girl was naked and was tied up. Livinus couldn't withstand the sight; he immediately made use of a heavy object that he was able to find around and broke into the house. He untied the young girl and discovered that she was already at the point of death; no need to question what would have happened because the whole evidence was there. The plate still having the content of some pepper was still on the floor, and the iron beside it with two well knotted "koboko." The overall bleeding back is enough suggestion that the iron was used on her. Immediately, Livinus zoomed off in a way the antelope runs from the lion in search of a taxi. Luckily, he was able to find one on time, and with the help of the taxi driver, they immediately rushed her to a nearby hospital.

"The people wey do this get heart o," the driver had said.

On arriving at the hospital, the attention of the doctor was called on. The doctor seeing the condition of the young Chizoba immediately swung into action with his band of nurses. It took divine intervention for the young Chizoba to see again. After four days, the eyes managed to open but not without defect; the pain was still there. The worst was that she had become short-sighted, a myopic tendency that had made her lack vision. She can only see things that are at a close range, where far things appeared so blurred to her. Despite the fact that she has been on so many injections to lessen the pain, she is yet to recover from it. The pepper burn is no more but not without a scare, but the iron burn, which is always a scar she will carry for the rest of her life, is still very painful because it is fresh. She would always lay on her stomach because it is practically impossible for her to do so with her back.

The doctor had asked Livinus what happened to the girl. He had told him of how he came to work in the morning as was usual with him, only to hear her shouting. Though he took it to be a usual occurrence because he always does hear her cries every time he is there. Of how he had gone to check on her when her guardians had left the house, only to find her in such pitiable condition, and had her rushed to the hospital. It was only on the fifth day that Chizoba was able to narrate what actually had happened to her. Chizoba woke up and was confused about her whereabouts. She took a careful look and noticed she was in a hospital. How she got to the hospital was still far from her remembrance. She started crying again when she woke up.

On seeing that she had finally opened her eyes, the nurse on duty, in an elated mood, immediately rushed to the doctor's office to tell him the good news. The doctor received the news with happiness and at once headed to the emergency ward to see her. The doctor asked her if she could remember anything that happened, but it seemed she had lost her memory of sort. It was after five days in the hospital that she was able to recall what had happened. The day was very hectic for me, and I was sick but wasn't given any medicine. After going to bed around 2 am after my aunties children had slept, I still had to wake up by 5 o'clock in the morning as usual to accomplish my daily morning function. I had to bathe

the children, sweep the compound, mop the floor, and get the breakfast ready. After doing that, I went to the market to buy the items with which I used to cook "oha soup" for the afternoon meal. After cooking the soup, I also had to cook the groundnut, which I was supposed to hawk for the day, and set off to the market. During the afternoon, I had come home to make "eba," which would be used to eat the soup for lunch, set the food on the dining table, and had my madam informed. Not that she isn't always around, but I do everything in the house; even when I want to do things before time, she wouldn't allow me, so every day, I do come back to make lunch.

So, after making the lunch for the day, I went back to the market to continue my sales because I was severely beaten any day I fail to finish the basket of groundnut. Since hawking was the only choice I was left with after being withdrawn from school, I had come to love the business, knowing so well that that's what the future holds for me and nothing better than that. When I returned in the evening, I was beaten mercilessly as usual because I was unable to finish the heap of groundnuts my madam had sent me to sell because there was no market. After crying for a while, I had to wipe my tears. I bathed the babies and entered the kitchen to make food for the night, knowing fully well that failure to do so would attract even heavier punishments for me as had always been the case.

I finished cooking around 8 pm, which was when I had my first meal for the day. I was forbidden to eat anything food in the house except supper. Formerly I was allowed to eat twice daily but have been eating once for the past seven weeks. After I had finished eating, my madam called me to come and carry the kids so she could go to sleep. I obtained permission from her to quickly round off the used dish I was washing. She was very angry and barked at me, so I did everything fast so as not to incur her wrath for the night.

After washing the dishes, I quickly took my bath, rushed, and carried the little children. My madam handed over the bottled breast milk to me as she normally does on a daily basis and retired for the day. Both babies were crying; I had tied one on my back and carried the other on my hands. They were crying, so I had to walk the whole room singing different lullabies to lure them to sleep because they kept crying anytime I tried sitting down. When it was already three o'clock in the morning, I finally had to sit down without them waking up and crying. As I was sitting down on the sofa, sleep took control of me, and in the process, the baby I was carrying in my hands slipped and fell.

I woke up on hearing my madam shout. My Madam, on witnessing the happening, gave out a loud shout which made me stand immediately on my feet. She left me with a strong slap and rushed over to her son. She ran an inspection and miraculously and luckily for me, nothing happened to him. It took up to ten minutes before I could recover from the mesmerizing effect of the slap. She untied the baby on my back and carried her children to her husband's room.

I thought all was over until around eight o'clock in the morning. After cooking the day's groundnut, I was preparing to leave for the market when both madam and my oga stormed my room with "koboko" and iron in their hands. On seeing the "koboko," I already knew it was for me but couldn't envisage the mission of the iron. They stripped me stark naked, and each armed with a "koboko," started showcasing the only thing they know how to do best. After beating me to their satisfaction, they plugged and had the electric iron heated. They laid me on the floor and started pressing my back with the iron. My cries and agony rented the air, but none of them cared; instead, they both were wearing a happy face.

After smearing my back with the iron, my madam headed straight to the kitchen and reappeared with a plate of pepper in her hand. She rubbed some of the pepper in my eyes. The husband helped to spread my legs while my madam started inserting the remaining pepper into my private part. The pain was so unbearable to me, and it seemed I passed out because I can't remember anything that happened next. After hearing her stories, the doctor was so touched, he couldn't imagine the kind of heart that some have. Just imagine a thirteen-year-old girl taking care of two children and keeping awake till 3 am.

"How did I get here?" asked Chizoba. The doctor explained to her everything that happened, of how she was brought to the hospital by one Livinus and a taxi driver. Chizoba couldn't be less grateful.

"Where is the man now?" she asked.

"He went home not quite long but will be here tomorrow as he has always been doing," the doctor replied. Looking at her condition, Chizoba couldn't help but burst into tears. So, this is how her City experience had come to be. She wouldn't have believed if a diviner had foretold this because, in her wildest imagination, she still couldn't believe that Nneka is such a heartless devil. She recalled her first day in the City, of how she was warmly welcomed, taken out for sightseeing, and enrolled in the best school. How on earth would she have imagined that she will end up a dropout and a graduated groundnut seller?

It took the effort of the doctor to stop her from crying.

"Please stop crying, my dear; I believe God knows why all this happened. He created the whole universe and everything in it, and no one questions His authority. As the architect of the cosmos, He holds the structural design and orders the happening of things. So, in all situations, whether good or bad, we ought to return all praises to Him, who is the alpha and omega, for He knows why. You should be thanking God for having kept you alive. I believe He still has something in store for you, for Him to have sent you a helper and didn't allow the gruesome cold hands of death to glue you." The picture of the young Chizoba was already in circulation on the internet. In a bid to get financial assistance from people, photos of the young Chizoba were taken and uploaded on social media platforms. It became the most viewed due to the caption they gave it. It was captioned:

"THE LITTLE GROUNDNUT SELLER HAS BEEN KILLED, BUT A VIEW COULD WAKE HER."

The caption alone attracted many viewers; people were all wondering how on earth a view can wake a dead person.

"Journalists sef," one of the viewers had commented.

Many people were against the inhumane act meted against the girl. Everyone was demanding justice for the little girl. Well-meaning individuals were already making donations to save her life. Things took a different turn when the Governor of the State came to know about what had happened. His media aide had brought the matter to his attention. On seeing the pictures, the governor broke into tears. "Is this an animal or a human?" he asked.

"It's a human that was treated like an animal," the aide replied. The Governor cried, seeing this height of man's inhumanity to man. The following day, he and his entourage stormed the "God Heals General Hospital" to confirm the authenticity of the news. Seeing the young Chizoba even made the governor cry the more. He asked for the details, and Chizoba told him everything from scratch; how she came to live with her aunt in the City after the death of her father owing to their poor nature. She told him of how good they were to her at first, how they enrolled her to Urban Community Secondary School, and how everything changed after the death of her mother, starting from her being withdrawn from school to selling groundnut in the market, of how she became a sexual bait and was always taken advantage of by her madam's husband and how life had been so hard for her.

The governor told her not to worry, that everything would be all right, at least that she's already in safe hands and won't go back to suffering. He promised her that he would never rest until the wicked perpetrators are brought to book. There and then, he brought out his phone and dialed the commissioner of police, giving him the address given by Chizoba; he ordered him to immediately go down to Big Brothers Estate and effect the arrest of one Mr. and Mrs. Ukadike with immediate effect. He also called the State's Attorney General, informing him of the pending course. According to him, justice must be served.

He instantly adopted Chizoba as his own daughter right away and assured her that her days of suffering were over and that he would do everything within his power to ensure her bright future. He gave her a lifetime scholarship. Before going, the Governor cleared the hospital bill and informed the doctor of his intent to move her to another hospital where she would be better treated. Then next week, the young Chizoba was flown abroad for surgery and for better medical attention.

The commissioner did not waste time in carrying out the arrest. Not long had the Governor hung up, had he plunged his men into action. He led the way, and they started off to the Big Brothers Estate with five Hilux vans filled with armed policemen. Anybody that saw them and how fast they drove wouldn't require the assistance of a soothsayer to tell that deep trouble loomed for the person they were in search of. Ukadike and his family were already prepared to fly out of the country. They already saw the news making the rounds and had planned to avert the consequences of their actions. To show their level of wickedness, they never gave a damn when they had returned and found the door open with Chizoba nowhere to be found. They instead continued their normal lives.

Nature had a way of boomeranging actions. On that night that Chizoba was taken to the hospital, Chinazaek-pere fell sick and gave up the ghost before dawn. Nneka and her husband cried so hard. Their only comfort still remained the fact that they still had one, but just as the Igbo's will say, "A one-eyed man owes a great debt to blindness." Thank God the baby did not die in the hands of Chizoba; who knows what would have happened to her if such had happened. She was left in a critical manner just because a child slipped from her hand and fell without sustaining an injury, and thank God it wasn't Chukwudi that died.

"Honey, please be fast; we have a flight to catch," Ukadike called out. "I'm almost through, sweetheart."

They had gotten everything ready when unfortunately for them, the armed troop arrived. All the inhabitants of the estate who were still in the house at that time had come out to behold the scenario. None of them knew what was happening or whom the policemen had come to visit. Some had it that maybe they visited a top-ranking officer in the estate, while others speculated that maybe an arrest was to be made. Their guess was straightened when the vehicles pulled and came to a halt in front of the eleventh building.

"Serves them right," one of the neighbors had said, confirming her guess.

"Every day is for the thief, but one day is for the owner; it seems they have met their waterloo," she had said. It was Silas's wife.

She seemed to be the happiest among the spectators. At least her husband and the innocent Chizoba will be placated.

Almost everybody in the neighborhood was happy when they learned that one of her babies died. Though death is a painful thing, and one needs not to rejoice at the death of another, but some deaths are explained to be intertwined with karma. Karma has a way of paying back in the law of gravitation. Indeed, anything that goes up must surely come down; since we are not out of space, and what goes around comes around. People had interpreted the death of the young girl as payback by nature. Certainly, you can't intend to kill someone's child and let yours live for you; something must happen in a way, if not now then later, but definitely something must happen.

Save the fact that Ukadike was already outside when the men arrived; he would have tried running or even tried something stupid. But the sudden arrival of the men caught him unawares.

"You must be Mr. Ukadike Chukwuemeka," the commissioner asked him.

"Yes, and to what do I owe this visit?" he asked in reply.

"I'm Mr. Ibrahim Mohammed, the State Commissioner of Police," he said and, without pausing, continued.

"You are under arrest for the attempted murder and inhumane treatment meted on one Miss Uwadiegwu Caroline Chizoba; you have the right to remain silent, for anything you say now will be used against you in the court of law."

Ukadike was perplexed. He felt that the earth should just swallow him. He knew serious trouble was looming, for the Commissioner to have come for the arrest himself was a clear pointer that it was indeed a serious matter. "We can settle this amicably commissioner, you and your boys should come inside and let me offer you some kola. I have got loads of money, and I'm ready to give you anything; please just name your price," He pleaded.

"Mr. Man, do you think we are here to joke or for child's play?"

"And if I got what you just said right, you are trying to bribe the officer of the law and distort justice?"

"Mind you, you are on record," said the Commissioner.

"This is money we are talking about; please, I can offer you all three million each."

"I'm on my way now to the United States; just make the news that I escaped, please."

"Corporal handcuff this useless man, let's get out of here," the commissioner ordered in a thunder-like manner.

Ukadike was immediately handcuffed and pulled into the vehicle. Nneka, who knew not what was going on, had come out with Chukwudi so they could leave immediately. On coming out, and on beholding the already gathered crowd, she tried to rush back inside the house and was given a hot chase by one of the policemen. In the process of trying to run with her heels on, she slipped and fell on top of her child.

Turning and turning in a widening gyre!

The innocent swallowed up in wickedness,

A path not chosen, but nature calls.

Blood drips!

Pool formed!

The succulent crashed in innocence;

With a breath gone to the creator.

The worst has just happened as a drip of blood had already formed a pool. The little Chukwudi had crashed his head on the floor, dying instantly. The mood of sorrow had rented the air. The sight is not only terrifying but an eyesore. The twins had gone back to their creator. Despite the incident, she and her husband were taken away amidst different curses and abuses on them by the neighbors and on-lookers. Nothing goes so fast in life like news because each witness is already a carrier, and he or she goes around infecting each person they come across, and within a short period, it will no longer be news as everybody will know about it.

Various newspapers and social media platforms carried the news of the incident. It had indeed become the talk of the town. Even those born today know the story of the uncovered wickedness. Only if they knew a day like this would come when justice would develop a fast-running leg and overtake them. The nemesis of their wickedness had caught up with them.

"THE DEVIL HAD BEEN TAKEN AWAY AND A DOWNTRODDEN ANGEL RESCUED."

The above was one of the captions making the rounds. Later, the case was charged to court, and both Ukadike and his wife were sentenced to ten years imprisonment with hard labor; on account of the charge of attempted murder, inhumane treatment, attempted bribery, and distortion of the law. The couple had cried so bitterly.

"You caused this," Ukadike blamed the wife.

"You lured me into becoming your accomplice, a very bad woman you are."

"I can't stop cursing the day I met you."

Ukadike and Nneka were dragged into the "Black Maria" and taken away to the prison. People were so happy about these developments. The young Chizoba had finally been vindicated. The young Chizoba had been flown abroad for treatment with a lifetime scholarship while the wicked souls rot in jail.

CHAPTER TWELVE

Dr. Bethram, as he was fondly called by his associates, is a handsome, tall, broad-shouldered, fair young man. He had a cherubic face and wore an Afro hairstyle, which further accentuated his gentility and elegance. Bethram was so handsome and a good-looking man that it was rumored in the past that while pregnant with him, his mother had an encounter with the angel of beauty.

Stories had it that Ukemma was on her way to the market when she had the one-on-one encounter. The angel had gone in search of who to bless. On sighting Ukemma, the angel immediately found favor in her and decided to possess her unborn baby. The child would have been a girl, but jealousy arose among the female angels, who feared being rivaled in beauty and grandeur by any human. This generated a whole lot of tension in the sky because it is far impossible to undo the deeds of the angel of beauty, for any otherwise attempt will end up leaving both the angel and the child dead. After several meetings and consultations aimed at restoring peace among them, God then decided to turn the baby into a boy to avert the imminent violence looming in His kingdom, for no matter how handsome a man is, he can never be as elegant as the female angels.

How time flies, that baby of yesteryears had now grown into a man. It had not been long he returned from overseas. Bethram was sitting on a tree branch outside the house, receiving fresh air when two lovers had passed in a romantic mood. "What a nice set of lovers, how I wish I can have such luck," he said.

Relationships have indeed not been favorable to him. Despite his handsomeness and affluence, a steady and stable relationship had been a problem for him. He doesn't know why people always see him as a cheat, despite the fact that he never cheated in a relationship. It's crystal clear that what the girls really want is his money and not necessarily because of love, maybe because they noticed that his previous relationships didn't last, and they just came to enjoy his money while it lasted.

He remembered Precious Ogechukwu, a girl he had developed strong feelings for during his secondary school days. He tried everything possible in wooing the lady only for her to break his heart. Although it was his only relationship that was intended to last, his hope had been dashed. He came back to find out she had long been married with three kids. He seriously blamed himself for not maintaining communications with her. How they came to date was still very fresh in his memory. Bethram was indeed a shy type and had stopped her on the way on several occasions only to lose his speech. He could remember the first time he mustered the courage to meet her and talk things face to face. He was indeed a football lover those days and had attempted a strike in one of their matches with a visiting school.

The time that Thursday was ten o'clock or thereabout. Students of University secondary school had just arrived at Benefits International Secondary School, their own school, for the long-awaited football match, in respect of the federal government schools football competition. They were singing different kinds of football chants and drumming as they drove in. Others were basking in the euphoria of the band-beat.

The crescendo of their chants swallowed all the noises in their host school, thereby making everybody, including Benefit students, completely absorbed in the rhythm, giving more voice to the sayings that music is a universal language, and not only that but food to the soul. It was really an interesting scene.

After they drove around the field, the driver finally pulled the bus to a stop. As they were alighting from the bus, they carried with them a big "Ghana must go" bag containing their team jerseys and boots. Apart from their musical instruments, they also carried bags of sachet water, chewing gums, and containers of glucose.

Before their arrival, Benefit players were already on the field training and waiting for their visitors. Immediately the visiting school arrived, they wore their kit quickly and proceeded to the field. As soon as the University secondary players settled down at one end of the arena, both players and supporters of the host school started greeting their visitors as it's customary before the start of a competition. The greetings usually come in the form of handshakes.

Bethram being one of the key players had long waited for this day. On sighting Precious, his mind had skipped.

Bethram, who had always played in the first half of the game, had resolved to play in the second. There was tension as this did not go down well with the other players.

"Guy, this is a competition that we have long been training for," they protested in persuasion.

At last, they were reshuffled. What brought about Bethram's sudden change of mind and strange behavior during the selection of the players baffled many people; even Francis, his friend, was not left out. This was a person that had trained so hard to "Ronaldo-standard." Bethram, before this day, already said he was going to score just two against their opponents, so why the change of mind now. When the match had started, Bethram quietly excused himself from the team. On noticing his sudden disappearance, Francis went in search of him.

Being his best friend, it was only he that knew something was not that cool with him. He was in the canteen with a bottle of Coca-Cola in his hand when Francis saw him.

"Bethram, so you are here?" Francis asked in a confrontational manner, looking quizzically into his friend's eyes.

"Have you been looking for me?" he replied with a question.

"For long now."

"Anything the matter?" Bethram asked, trying to wear a new look.

"Stop pretending and tell me what your problem is," Francis fired.

"I left the field in search of you because I knew that something was troubling your heart. Besides, you look very worried. Tell me what the problem is and free your mind so that we can leave for the match, for there is no time."

"Francis, nothing is my problem, or do you pray I have one?" he queried.

"Stop telling me that nothing is amiss. Bethram, nothing is amiss while you no longer associate with anybody?"

"Nothing is amiss while you stay so quiet like a mourning widower?"

"I don't know what you are talking about, dear," Bethram answered in defense.

"Look! If you are not ready to tell me what has been troubling you, then I think it's high time I left," Francis said and went his way.

He deliberately refused to reveal the cause of his emotional turmoil. He had resolved to confront precious, at least, to express his never-dying feelings.

"I must not reveal this to Francis now. He must know, but at least, not now. He would call me a wayward boy or laugh at me if I'm turned down. The truth is that I cannot play football today. Let me face what is facing me. I must say at least a hello to her today," he muttered to himself.

The match had entered the second half since the past twenty minutes, and yet Bethram was nowhere to be found. He was in a hidden place. He tried to sight Precious among other girls that clustered on the fringes of the field as they were cheering their players who were performing gallantly. It was really a tough match. Both teams were doing well. But only the god of soccer would decide who would gain the upper hand. It was when one heavy corner-kick, played by their opponent, descended on the crowd that Bethram sighted her. Without hesitation, he sent one girl to fetch her.

"Do you see that tall browned-skin girl with a curvy body and a pointed nose over there?" Bethram described pointing his finger at her.

"Do you mean Precious?" the girl asked.

"Yeah, do you know her?"

"Of course, she is my classmate," the girl responded.

"Please, help me and call her; I am waiting for you here," he pleaded. Bethram was happy that the canteen was very serene as people had all gone to the field for the match. At least he will be the only one to bear the grave shame in case of a negative outcome. As he sat for a while, he heard some footsteps coming in his direction. He abruptly repositioned himself with the hope that they were the people coming. But to his ultimate disappointment, it was two little boys coming towards him. In a rage, he ordered them to go back to the field immediately. As a senior student, they obeyed him without complaint.

Soon after, the girl came into the company of Precious and excused herself.

"Good afternoon, "Precious greeted.

"Same here, dear," he replied, his face beaming with a smile like that of a hungry lion that saw a lamb drinking by the waterside.

"I can see you are watching the match," was what came out of his mouth after all he had practiced.

"Yes," she answered unconcernedly.

"Why not go and join your colleagues in the field," she said.

"Did anybody tell you that I was one of the players?" he asked her.

"Are you not the Bethram I see every day in the field?"

"Please, forget about football stuff; let us discuss an important business."

"Which funny business?"

"Please, I don't think I have any business with you," Precious replied with an intention to leave but had to stay on second thought.

Precious, please, why can't you give me at least three seconds to express my feelings for you?" he sounded soft in his approach.

"OK, what do you want from me?"

"Since last term when I was sent to invigilate your class during a test, I was opportune to see you, and since then, my heart has never had any rest. I think I'm madly in love with you. My unadulterated love for you is growing uncontrollably day by day," he answered as if being interviewed by his boss. "OK, Mr. Lover boy, if I may ask, what do you love about me?"

"I love the way you look; I love the way you talk and the way you walk. In short, I love everything about you," he paused.

"Everything is really nothing, so why else do you love me?" she asked.

Bethram paused for a while before continuing; seriously, he didn't know it was going to be this hard. He wanted to run, but that would be an indelible insult to his personality, so he continued. "It is just for three reasons and reasons which every rational man will find in any woman who is worthy of being embraced. Firstly, you are so beautiful; you are well behaved, and you are intelligent. In fact, I lack real explanation and would wallow vainly in a futile word-seeking attempt to perfectly explain how and what I love about you."

"Thanks for your admiration; I think I want to go," she implored.

"I know you really want to go, but what is your opinion on this issue?" he asked politely.

"I will think about it," she said and left.

"Excuse me, at least let me get you something to go with," Bethram uttered, but she resisted.

Immediately, a hilarious shout was heard, and the echo rebounded through all the nooks and crannies of the school premises. It was them that had scored one goal, just two seconds to the end of the match. It was through a penalty kick played by Francis who had replaced him with the number ten jersey. Before the ball could be passed again, the referee stopped the game. Everywhere was painted red with dust as the entire Benefit students rose, jubilating over their victory. Bethram was neither happy nor angry because of his encounter with Precious,

"I should think about it is not a bad idea anyway, at least I finally relayed my feelings to her. I just pray it will end in praise," he told himself. He joined his team in singing victory songs. Thank God they won; if not, the game master would have killed him that day. Later on, Precious had given her consent, and that was how their relationship started.

"That was then when Obi was still a boy?" he smiled to himself.

He remembered his friend Francis and sighed. Francis had died in a motor accident during his final year in the university. He was on his way walking home after his project defense when a car hit him from the back, leaving him dead at the spot. As is the case with hit-and-run drivers, the driver immediately fled with no trace. It was indeed a painful death as all the resources that were spent to train him had been in vain since certificates are not transferable.

"We are still living by His grace and not ours," he sighed again. Bethram was still deeply pained by her marital development. He was shocked to the marrow to know of it. It is indeed a surprise of nature to a man that someone we meet on a random basis could turn to be part of us to the extent that we can't think of our life without them.

"I would have married her."

"But it wasn't her fault in a way because communication is of the essence for the success of any relationship."

"I think I should just find a girl and marry now to avoid all this heartbreak, she has moved on, and it's already too late to do anything now," he said.

His parents had been on his neck to marry for a long time. As the only child of the family, they had considered him marrying early to avoid any story that touches the heart; God forbid should anything happen to him. "He needs to marry and bear children, especially a male child, to perpetuate my lineage," his father had suggested.

The tension generated the day he told his parents of his intention of first finishing his masters abroad before thinking of marriage had been saved at the back of his mind. In the night after his national youth service, when their visitors had all departed, his parents had called him into their inner room to talk about the same thing that had always been giving them sleepless nights.

"I think it's high time you take a wife since your education which you have been using as an excuse, is over," the father said. When Bethram told them that he still had to finish his housemanship before thinking of settling down, his mother was very much angered and disappointed.

"Which one is housemanship again?"

"It's now obvious you don't want me to carry my grandchildren before I walk among the dead," she complained.

"How many weeks is it going to take?" retorted his father.

"One year, papa," he replied.

"I can see that they have finally succeeded in brainwashing you; little wonder I rarely see you with a girl since you attained maturity," Mr. Eugene provocatively spoke. Mr. Eugene, by the standard, is a wealthy merchant. He took an interest in education when he was insulted with big grammar by the son of a fellow businessman, and since that day, he had sworn to himself that he would train Bethram up to the university level as opposed to his wish of marrying him a wife immediately after his secondary school. Being his only son and regarding his affluence, Bethram already had a car in secondary school and never experienced any form of hardship.

"Seems like I over-pampered this boy," he said.

But all is in the past now; he had already finished his housemanship and is now a certified medical doctor. Being burdened with thought, he dialed Samson, his friend, so that they could go and get some fun. Bethram later opened his hospital amidst great joy from friends and well-wishers. The hospital was named EUGENE'S MEMORIAL HOSPITAL; In memory of his father, who was late before his arrival.

"I will forcefully get you a wife soon," Ukemma whispered to his ear in the middle of the party, and both laughed hysterically. It was really a good time for mother and son, as they partied with numerous others present.

CHAPTER THIRTEEN

The hospital was very busy; there were too many patients, and the doctor was very busy from morning till about 3 pm when he got exhausted and wanted to go for a break. Dr. Bethram came out to the general outpatient department (GOPD) to announce that he was going for a thirty-minute break to continue later. It was the turn of a pretty lady, chocolate in color and had attractive eyes. On sighting the girl, he was charmed by her beauty and instead announced that he was going to see one more person in the queue before proceeding for the break as opposed to his earliest intention. He went back to his office and rang the bell, which is an indication for a patient to enter.

The young lady, taking cognizance of an old man in the queue, went to him and asked him to enter, knowing quite well that it would be very difficult for him to wait till the expiration of the break. In the office, Dr. Bethram had already positioned himself to talk to this beautiful lady when the door creaked open, revealing an old man. His countenance changed immediately by this unexpected appearance, but he had no choice but to attend to the old dude.

When Bethram came, after seeing five persons, it became the supposed turn of the old man whom the young lady had replaced after she granted her position to him. Dr. Bethram was surprised because he was not expecting to see the girl again whom he thought might have gone.

"What happened?"

"You were the person I was expecting to see before proceeding on a break as I observed during my announcement; how come I saw someone instead?" Bethram asked, still surprised. "Yes, but it could have been too stressful for that elderly man, so I decided to take his turn," she responded.

"Wow, that's so kind of you."

"What is your name, and where are you from," he asked.

"My name is Dr. Uwadiegwu Caroline Chizoba, and I'm from Amaokwu; somewhere in Enugu State," she replied

"What about you?" Chizoba asked.

"I'm Dr. Bethram Emeka Ihedioha from Ikwuato village in Anambra State.

"Nice meeting you."

"It's my pleasure," she replied.

"What can I do for you?" Dr. Bethram asked.

"I was sent to deliver this to you by the Governor," she said, handing him an envelope.

Dr. Bethram was so shocked knowing that this same girl that gave up her place for an old man was not even sick or had been diagnosed with any illness but had come to deliver a message from the governor himself and had been on the queue since then instead of walking majestically into his office as is the expected norm among the people. Though her intonation and choice of words suggest a person that attended a standard school, he still asked to know the school she graduated from to know if she had attended a cheap school that made her well-mannered or naive.

"I graduated from Harvard Medical School in the United States," came her reply. Immediately, everything in Dr. Bethram's body jumped up. It was then he knew he was with a high personality. He stood and requested a handshake.

"I graduated from our university here, but I did my masters in London," Bethram told her in-between the handshake. After a short conversation, Chizoba stood to go.

"Here's my complimentary card; please try and give me a call anytime," he offered her with a broad smile. Chizoba gave him hers and left. As the door closed, Bethram unconsciously stood up and excitedly mumbled, "Yes! I have seen my wife. I pray to God that she must not have been betrothed to anybody."

After seeing patients for the day, he immediately rushed home and didn't branch anywhere to catch some fun as he used it to cover up if he was to go drink. On reaching home, without wasting any atom of time, he called on his mother immediately. On pronouncing his intention to her, his mother rushed to and jumped on top of him, making mother and son fall down on the sofa. Ukemma was extremely happy about hearing the news. "Today is indeed the best of all my days," she exclaimed.

After telling his mother a few things about the girl, he told her he intends to settle down with the girl and that he's just praying that she would be single and accept him. His mother made a prayer point immediately. After informing her mom, he rushed back to his car and sped off to see his best friend, Samson. When he got to where Samson's was, he broke the news to him and instantly ordered drinks for them to start celebrating already.

"Barman," he called,

"Come and get this table loaded; the bill's on me," he said.

Samson, no doubt, is indeed an enemy that later turned friend. They became enemies after opposing each other in a school election; both had vied for the post of the director of transport. Though none of them won, they had become enemies after all. It was not until their service year that fate brought them together; they were posted to the same place for their national youth service program, and it was until then that both realized they were from the same state. Ever since then, they have become best of friends. Samson was a short fellow, but his social nature made him too endeared to the female gender. Ladies so much liked him hence the explanation for his promiscuity. He can wonderfully be in three different relationships without knowing and making each of them feel so special. During their service year, Bethram had nicknamed him the great Solomon for his expertise in wooing women.

He was indeed overjoyed hearing that Bethram had finally gotten over Precious and had picked interest in another lady. On countless occasions, Bethram's mother tipped him to talk to her son, and none of his approaches yielded any fruit. He even had to pay a girl to seduce him, but it didn't work out. "So, tell me more about this, your new girl," Samson said after gulping a mouthful of beer.

Bethram, like a professional storyteller, immediately narrated everything as it happened to him. He spiced up the whole story to make Chizoba appear so profiled in Samson's imagination. On hearing that she schooled in Harvard, Samson already liked her. However, he was somehow disappointed hearing nothing concrete as regards intimacy between the duo.

"So, when are we going to meet her family?" asked Samson.

"That's why I have called you my friend; I really need your help on this, "he replied. You are my best friend, and you know your happiness is of utmost importance to me, so feel free to ask for anything."

"I need you to help me spy on this girl to know if she's seeing someone else already or betrothed to any fellow before I can make my move," Bethram appealed.

"Did she give you her address?"

"Yes, it's in the complementary card she gave me," he replied.

"Then you don't have any problem as regards that; I'm giving you my word. I will find out everything about her." Though Samson is a political scientist by profession, his prowess in spying on people is of great commend. After having their drinks, they resolved to carry out their plans from the following day.

Bethram could not wait up to 1:00 pm, his normal break hour, before going home to check if Samson had come up with anything positive. He had gone home twice, all to no avail. His mother had asked him if there was any problem, but he had given an excuse of having a running stomach. Ukemma already knew he was lying, knowing fully well that there are toilet facilities in his office. After his mother had caught him in the lie, he finally revealed why he had been coming home to her.

"Why not call him on the phone?" Ukemma suggested.

"His phone has been off throughout today, mama."

It's very unusual for Samson's phone to be off; an unprecedented happening, as was reasoned by Bethram. Samson finally called around 5 o'clock in the evening.

"How did it go?" he asked hastily.

"The eagle is perching on a branch where the hunter can effortlessly aim at it," Samson replied. "Common wise man speaks in a language your guy will understand, you know I'm not good with proverbs of any sort."

Samson gave him a detailed explanation of his discovery. Chizoba had been back for just two weeks and seemed not to be engaged to anyone. He told him she's a daughter of Honorable Obi, the former governor of their State. Bertram was so happy at this positive outcome. No one who knew them from their quarter years in school would have ever believed Samson could be of great help to him now as he is of immense help. Bertram was so happy within him that their relationship was not totally stalled by a somewhat myopic tussle of one-year office. He remembered a story one professor had told them about the Lion and the rat;

There was a terrible famine in the animal kingdom. One fateful day, the Lion set out in search of what to eat. He met the Rat, who was also looking for food. On sighting his prey, the Lion immediately gave a hot chase and grabbed her. In an attempt to swallow her, she begged him to have pity and save her for the fact that she was a nursing mother, and if he swallows her, her offspring will perish.

Moreover, she would not even satisfy him as little as she was. She finally told the Lion to spare her life, that tomorrow, she might be in a position to help him. The Lion broke into a peal of long laughter. He said to the Rat;

"I am only leaving you to go and wean your offspring, not that you could help me in any way. Look at you, how do you think you could offer me any sort of help, the lion?"

Three days later, as the Rat was going out to search for food, she saw a lion trapped. She looked closer and recognized him with his long mane to be the Lion she encountered some days back. She went closer to the scene. It was the traditional trap that was made of cable wire. Both his two hands and two legs were entangled. He looked very tired after much futile struggle for freedom. The Rat immediately swung into action and, after much tedious work, was able to cut the cables with her teeth. The lion was freed. He had stayed there for two days. He stood and looked at the rat and, with tears in his eyes, said to her, "I never knew that you could help me one day; without you, I would have died here."

Professor Thiago had always told these stories before any class to teach them the importance of maintaining good relationships, telling them that tomorrow is pregnant and no one knows what it will bear. Here is the story making meaning to him now about Samson. "The words of the wise live thousands of years with an unfolding meaning," he reasoned of Sir Thiago.

Bethram later opted for lunch with Chizoba, where he made known his intentions to her. As it's customary with the girl-folks, she objected at the initial stage even though she had come to love the young man, but after a little while of persistence from Bethram, she decided to give him a try.

Chizoba and Bethram started dating afterward and later got engaged. It was indeed a dream come true for both of them. Their love for each other knows no bounds and keeps increasing as the day goes. Chizoba had explained all her past to him and how she came to be adopted by the then governor. Bethram was so touched by the sad story. How on earth would someone have treated the love of his life in such absurdity, only if he could pay them back in their own coins for treating his wife in such a manner.

Four months into their dating, Bethram suggested they visit her village to know the current state of things since both her parents had died. Chizoba declined on the grounds that it will remind her much of her unpleasant past. Bethram tried everything possible to convince her so they could just have a look around the village. After many words of conviction, they later decided to go on the fortnight. Since her adoption, Chizoba had already erased everything about Amaokwu out of her mind. With the death of her father coupled with the injustice meted on them by the elders and finally the death of her mother, she had decided not to set her foot in Amaokwu throughout her stay on earth. She only accepted to visit for the last time just to make her husband happy.

"This will definitely be the last I will set my foot on that soil that once tormented my loved ones and me," she muttered inwardly to no one's hearing. Bethram was so happy she accepted his request. He made sure he cleared the work on his desk so as not to have any reason to disappoint. On the D-day, both lovers set out on Bethram's car en route to Amaokwu village.

It was a bright afternoon. Children were playing in the village square. That was how they played every Sunday. They normally do not go to farms. Though most of them did not go to church, they joined the Christians to observe the Sabbath day. The children were busy playing when suddenly, a dark jeep with tinted glasses zoomed into the playground. On seeing the children, the car slowed down. It was a brand-new jeep. The sound was not easily heard. It was the horn that made some of the children notice its presence. It really caught them unawares.

This kind of car hardly passed through their village. It was only Chukwuebuka, the Prince, that drove such a car in the entire village. On sighting the car, they relaxed, thinking it was the prince. Bethram stepped on the brake and rolled down the glass. When he beckoned on the children, they noticed it was a strange face and took to their heels.

There were rampant kidnapping cases in the village in the last two years, so they acted rather wisely. Some of their playmates had been victims of such. The criminals usually came in flashy cars, looking for human heads for ritual. They would sometimes pretend to have missed their way and seek direction to a particular place. They will decide to offer you a ride, and that will be your end. Or they might offer gifts to the children, and whoever collects will immediately turn into an inanimate object.

Parents had warned their children not to go to the village square to play. But that was two years back. They seemed to have forgotten that. Bethram and Chizoba were confused. They thought it to be a village mentality, but that was far from that. Such a conclusion amounts to the fact that Chizoba has had the village experience, too, so she didn't waste time in proposing the suggestion.

As the children ran without looking back, he decided to go further. At a point, he caught up with a woman who was also walking at a quickened pace when she saw the car coming after her. He turned off his car engine and tendered a mild greeting. The woman responded with fear written in her tone.

"Who are you?" she questioned, trying hard to muster courage.

"I'm Dr. Bethram. I am looking for Mr. Dike Uwadiegwu's residence. I suppose you know him.

The woman later took them to Dike's compound and immediately left as fast as her heels could carry her, even declining the tip Bethram wanted to offer her. Had she seen a girl in the car or a familiar face, her mind would have been at rest. But here is a man she had never seen in her life. Even Chizoba's face wouldn't have been familiar too.

Seeing the compound made Chizoba sob. A place full of memories. Nothing had really changed. The four huts were still there but now look smaller in her eyes. They decided to tour around the house when suddenly Chizoba sighted a familiar face from a distance. She was startled as the face became more familiar with each step closer. Behold, it was Christabel. Christabel, on sighting Chizoba, immediately rushed and threw herself at her. Both were very happy seeing each other again after a long period of time.

Christabel is already married with two kids and had visited in the company of her husband. They did a friendly introduction. Christabel had told her during their secondary school days that she's from Amaokwu, but seeing her in her father's compound is something she is yet to understand. What piled up the confusion is even the fact that they bear the same surname. Christabel, on the other hand, is not left out of the confusion. However, her father had told her that she had a lost elder sister, but she could not understand the game playing out. Both were engulfed in their discussion when an old man walked-in in the company of a woman suspected to be in her early fifties. Christabel introduced them as her father and mother.

"You are so lucky to still have your parents all alive; mine are late," Chizoba told her. "So sorry for your loss, dear," Christabel and her husband simultaneously said. They were offered kola and given a warm welcome. Despite the fact that the huts were still there, Chizoba was no longer certain considering the happenings. Maybe they have been directed to a wrong compound, she had reasoned. She asked Christabel for directions to Mr. Dike's compound and was more confused when she pointed to the old man as Mr. Dike.

"I was not opportune to meet my father; he died some days before my birth, as I was told, "Chizoba told her. Christabel immediately invited her father to know if he could help her friend with the direction she seeks. On hearing her out, Dike broke into deep tears.

"Could this be Adanma's daughter?" he said.

"Yes," Chizoba answered even though the question was not directed to her. At least she had seen someone that even knew her mother; maybe he can help give her a perfect direction. Dike reached out and hugged her so tightly amidst a great sob. Chizoba, in her wildest imagination, could not fathom out what was happening.

"I'm Dike, your father, and Adanma was my wife," he said, creating a tense atmosphere.

He narrated how he had gone into the bush on that fateful day and had mistakenly touched the "nju-leaf," which made him wander so far to an unknown land. Due to his inability to locate his way home, he finally settled there, where he married Miriam, Christabel's mother, and had given birth to Christabel and her two brothers - Tayo and Ibrahim. He later made wealth through the help of Miriam's father, who was a wealthy merchant and had come back to Amaokwu some years back to hear about the death of Adanma and had done everything possible in search of her.

Chizoba could not believe her ears. Blood has a very strong way of connecting. How would she have believed that the girl she had known all this while was her blood sister? Tears of joy rented the ear at this great union. Even Bethram and Christabel's husband were not left out of the joyous cry. People from the neighborhood had already started gathering. Chizoba told her stories amidst tears, and all present were shocked by such inhumane treatment melted on her by Nneka and her husband.

Dike immediately rushed and slaughtered the choicest of his goats in celebration. He thanked the gods for having availed him the opportunity of seeing this great day; at least he can now join his ancestors in peace. All thanks to Bethram, who had initiated this visit; if not, such a reunion wouldn't have been possible.

A date was later fixed for the marriage ceremony between Chizoba and Bethram. The marriage ceremony was no doubt the talk of the century. In fact, it was attended by the whole world. Many dignitaries were in attendance, including Ukadike and Nneka, who had been released from the prison some months back. After the wedding,

Ukadike and Nneka went to Chizoba and knelt down for forgiveness. After much pleading, they were forgiven. Chizoba later gave birth to twins, a boy and a girl, and named them Chinazaekpere and Chukwudi in memory of the late ones, and they lived happily ever after.

After some years, Chizoba has refused her ordeal, holding her back, and has used it to forge a successful career as a medical doctor and a Domestic Violence advocate while she fights for tougher legislative positions to tackle sexual predators, dehumanization, and maltreatment of women and young children.

In 2013, she set up a foundation named Chizoba Smart Foundation (CSF) which supports the indigent, women, and children who have suffered one form of abuse or the other. Her foundation serves as a rehabilitation and skill acquisition/ vocational center for some of them who want to learn skills. Currently, she partners with the state government in giving scholarships and empowerment to these women and children.

EPILOGUE
THERE'S STILL HOPE!!

Grace finds us when we are restless and in great pain. Grace comes when we swallow insults like medicine. Grace comes when the people we see as our champions have yet again broken us to our knees. Grace speaks when you just can't take anymore! It strikes when we walk through the valley of empty and meaningless life…… It strikes when on a daily basis, the longed-for perfection does not appear when our old hurt abides with us, as they have for so long. When despair destroys all joy and courage you have, GRACE SPEAKS!!! The Lord said, "My grace is sufficient for you." "For it's not yet over, it's not finished, it's not ending, and it's just the beginning when God is in it. God's grace is greater than all; trust in Him with all your heart and lean not on your own understanding; in all your ways acknowledge Him, and He shall direct your path."

There are women who have been through trouble, domestic violence, abuse, negligence, maltreatment, suffering, and torture, but they didn't allow all those troubles to deter them from achieving their purpose in life. Stay glued as we take out time to review the likes of these women, their early stage, the battles they fought and won, the stigmatization, and their survival testimonies.

Mabinty Bangura (Michaela DePrince) is an embodiment of what it means to fight for your dream. She didn't let anything stop her from becoming a professional ballerina, not her childhood, race, or vitiligo. Sierra Leonean-American Michaela DePrince was once a hopeless orphan at the age of three, nicknamed "the devil's child" because of the white dots that freckled her dark skin.

She was born in the African nation of Sierra Leone in the midst of a brutal civil war. Her parents died when she was a toddler, her father was shot, and her mother starved to death. Mabinty Bangura, then named Michaela, was sent to an orphanage by her uncle; he knew he'd never be able to get a bride price for her.

There, she was an outcast because of her vitiligo, a skin condition characterized by loss of pigmentation in certain places. In the orphanage, they kept saying, "Why would somebody want to adopt the devil's child?" At the orphanage, there were 27 children, and they were numbered. Michaela was number 27 and always got the smallest portion of food and leftover clothes. The aunties at the orphanage thought she was unlucky and evil because of her rare skin condition. She was too dirty. They braided her hair too tightly and wanted her to be in pain because they felt nobody will ever adopt her. Mabinty (Michaela) had a friend that was also called Mabinty, who made her happy by singing for her and telling her stories when she couldn't sleep. They slept on the same mat, and she was number 26.

Michaela thought she would never amount to anything good, then one day, she found a magazine outside the gate of the orphanage. On the cover was a picture of a ballerina in a tutu. She thought she was a fairy on her tippy toes in her beautiful pink costume. But what struck her most was that the ballerina looked so happy. Michaela hadn't been happy in a long time. She took the picture and hid it in her underwear.

At the orphanage, they had a teacher who came to teach them English lessons, and she showed her the picture. The teacher explained to her that the girl was a dancer. One day as they were walking together, some rebels came towards them. They had been drinking earlier and saw teacher Sarah with Michaela. Sarah was pregnant, and the rebels started arguing whether she was having a baby boy or girl. They thought they'd find out; they got their machete and cut her open. She was having a baby girl, so they killed both the teacher and her child in front of Michaela. They also cut Michaela's stomach too.

The rebels later threw all of them out and occupied the orphanage. They walked through the border to Guinea. There were plans for most of them to be adopted, and finally, there was a plane to Ghana. Michaela felt miserable because she thought she would never see her friend Mabinty again. To her surprise, a lady with blonde hair, which seemed amazing to her, and wearing bright red shoes grabbed her and her friend's hand too, and said: 'I'm your new momma.' That's how they became sisters.

When they got to the hotel, Michaela started looking through her new mother's luggage to find a tutu and pointe shoes because she thought all Americans were doctors, models, or ballerinas. She wasn't speaking English, so the only way she could explain what she was looking for was to bring out the picture she kept in her underwear, and her mother understood her outrightly. She told her she could dance if she wanted. She started going to ballet class when they got to America. Michaela found a video of Nutcracker and watched it more than 150 times. She begged her mom to take her to performance class, and by the time she clocked ten, she was going to ballet class five times a week. She became worried that the vitiligo on her skin would be a problem, but it turned out to be an issue in a different way. One of the ballet teachers told her mother that they don't put a lot of effort into the black girls, and they end up getting fat with big boobs. This made Michaela become strong and courageous. She had strength as a dancer, muscular, strong legs, and very hardworking. She was featured in the film "First Position," which followed six dancers preparing for the Youth American Grand Prix, a competition for places at elite ballet schools. She later got a place at Jacqueline Kennedy Onassis School. She kept on to her vision notwithstanding her condition. She was stigmatized as a child because of vitiligo, but it did not deter her from pursuing her vision and conquest.

To the readers out there, no matter what you are passing through, remember that God will give you a future and expected end, for His thought towards you is thought of peace and not of evil

Twahna was another survivor who was a sophomore in college. She fell in love with the wrong guy. She thought it was a perfect relationship till one day she felt his hand on her face, "Bitch if you had kept your mouth closed, it wouldn't have happened," he said. From that moment, her life turned upside down. She was mentally, emotionally, and sexually abused. He degraded her, talked about her being overweight, and stripped her of all her power. She began to question her self-worth, self-confidence, and her true purpose in life. She thought of suicide many times as a way out for her. She was too ashamed, embarrassed to share what she was going through with anybody. He isolated her from her support system, those who cared for her, lines of communication with family and friends, and monitored every move.

One day, Twahna eventually was courageous enough to tell a relative. She left him and went to live with her relative for a while, but her abuser convinced her to return to him. He swore he would seek counseling and an anger management program, but he never did. He lured her back with his sweet words and never changed a bit. He put his hands around her neck one day and began strangling her. It was like he was possessed. He said to her, "I will kill you if you ever leave again." She was dying in his hands. She went to bed that night and prayed, then heard the voice of God speak to her gently in her ear. She woke up the next morning and heard a voice say to her, "Today's the day you will leave." She couldn't believe her ears. She told him she was going to work and gave him a kiss. She went and hid behind a building across their apartment and waited until he left with his car. She returned to their apartment, gathered her things, and never returned.

She said it was the scariest moment of her life. Starting all over alone was challenging, but she pressed forward and determined to live again. She got busy volunteering at a local shelter and speaking out against domestic violence in some uncomfortable spaces. She returned back to the university and began dating again. She shared her story with a gathering of young women at an event remembering those who had lost their lives due to domestic violence. Her story impacted several of the women and was so inspiring even to her. She is the sole founder of Butterfly Society, which came into existence through her personal journey. They are the grass-roots organization-boost on ground, meeting people where they are, going to barber shops, neighborhoods, schools, and churches, educating, empowering, and engaging the community. She said, "One person can't do this alone. It takes many hands and many voices."

Kirby was another woman who didn't allow her circumstances to take over her dream and future. She wasn't perturbed about her situation, then later achieved her goals. Kirby met someone in high school, and they started dating. She became pregnant three months before their graduation and moved in with him because she wanted her daughter to have a father. He started beating her when she was pregnant, and the violence progressed. He treated her like she was a piece of his property, and nobody knew what happened behind closed doors. The abuse became sexual, physical, and emotional

Kirby later got her first restraining order after he came to her house, threw her around, and choked her. After four years, she got another one and dropped it because there was no one to represent her and his threats were terrible on her. She woke up in June 2017 and found him sexually assaulting her in her bed. She stood up and told him that what he was doing was rape. On hearing that, he threw her onto the bed, got on top of her, and started strangling her. She swung at him and bit him hard while her daughter yelled at him to stop.

She called the police, but they treated her like a delusional, hysterical, uncooperative person because she didn't want to repeat what she had already said four times in front of different men. The police report says she refused to write a statement, but she was never asked to do so. She was told she needed to decide if she would press charges of breaking and entering or call anybody that does rape kits. A police officer said her husband was being arrested for domestic abuse, battery, and strangulation. They said they were done handling her with kid gloves.

They called Child Protective Services on her for allowing their children to see spousal abuse. She was instructed to get a Protective Order for her and the kids. During the hearing, he was granted supervised visitation and required to take family violence intervention classes for twenty-six weeks. While he was taking the class, he got arrested four times yet got his certificate. After the class, he decided to file for sole custody of the kids. Kirby was so afraid he might kill her and the kids and flee to another country. He had a gun and a Glock fully loaded and well hidden in his garage, but Kirby was determined to fight him every step of the way.

Kirby, notwithstanding her challenges, co-founded VOICES of Acadiana, an organization that advocates for victims of domestic violence. Their mission is to advocate for victims of domestic violence by actively working towards systems change, educating and raising awareness around domestic violence, and survivor outreach to break the generational cycle of abuse. At Bayou church, a women's abuse group was set up, and Kirby broke her silence for the first time. Now she is a trained facilitator and shares her story in front of a group of over 160 women. She said, "It was an incredible feeling when these women stood up and clapped for me – it made me feel as though my chains were broken."

Dawn Johnson got an award of $15,000 through the Live Your Dream Award. She survived sexual and domestic abuse, and she is striving now to live her dreams with the assistance of Soroptimist's Live Your Dream Awards.

At 11, she entered the foster care system after enduring physical, emotional, and sexual abuse at home. She was introduced to prostitution and began using cracked cocaine at 12 (as it's always the case for girls who were sexually molested). By her 13years, the court mandated her to take part in a drug treatment program. She attempted suicide and later made three more attempts. She became a mother at 16 and got her life back on track for a while; then, things drastically changed when she ran away to live with her daughter's father. Living with her daughter's father was a living nightmare because he was an abusive alcoholic. One day, during a horrible argument at night, police took her from her home and took custody of their daughter. That incident served as a wake-up call to Dawn. She took a turn around in life for the better. She went back to school, sought help for her addictions, and was diagnosed with post-traumatic stress disorder brought on by years of abuse. She later began to heal gradually with counseling and support.

Within one year, her daughter was returned to her, and an agency asked Dawn to become a peer mentor. Through that position, she developed a passion for working with young people. Though she had dropped out of school in the 8th grade, she completed her course work and earned a diploma in child and youth care. She got involved in many youth advocacy programs and groups. The advice she gives to her girls is to always believe in themselves, that they are capable of anything.

Through the award of Live Your Dream, Dawn is helping to relieve some of the financial pressure she has raising two girls alone. It also helps her in continuing her education. Currently, she is pursuing a degree in child and youth care and has a plan to study law next. Continuing a law degree will give her the education and legal understanding to further advocate for those she works with. She said, "I take pride in being a strong and independent woman, but I have learned how to ask for help."

Lastly, the story of Oprah Winfrey is an encouraging one. She was born in Mississippi. Her mother Vernita moved north to Wisconsin to look for work and had plans of moving her young daughter with her after securing a good job. Oprah lived with her grandmother, who encouraged her to love books by teaching her how to read at the age of 3. She started by reading the Bible and began speaking at her church, then reciting Bible verses to her grandmother's friends. When she was six, she was sent to live with her mother and half-sister. Oprah was later sent to live with her father and stepmother Zelma in Nashville, Tennessee. They were happy to have her because they couldn't have children on their own. She was enrolled in Wharton Elementary School. Her parents took her to the library and valued her education. They attended church regularly, and she found more opportunities for public speaking even at her young age.

One day she turned on the television for company and had her first thoughts of being famous one day. She was nine years old when she was first sexually abused while babysitting Vernita's children. Her 19-year-old cousin raped her, took her out for ice cream, and told her to keep it a secret. She did, but it wasn't the end. Within the next few years, she faced more abuse from a family friend as well as an uncle. She kept silent about it all for years.

One of her teachers at Lincoln Middle School in downtown Milwaukee, Gene Abrams, took notice of her love for reading. He helped her transfer to an all-white school in Glendale, Wisconsin. She was very popular in the school because she was a black person.

Oprah was unable to talk to her mother about her sexual abuse, and her mother offered very little direction to the teenager. As a result, she started to act out. She was absent from school most times, dated boys here and there, stole money from her mother and ran away from home. Her mother couldn't handle her behavior for long, then sent her back to Nashville to live with her father. She realized she was pregnant when she was just 14. She hid the news from her parents until she was seven months gone, went into early labor, informed her father of the pregnancy the same day, and delivered a baby boy who later died two weeks after delivery.

Oprah had a turnaround when she turned 16 after reading Maya Angelou's autobiography, "I know why the Caged Bird Sings." The book transformed the teen's life, and she read it over and over again. The book validated her existence, and many years later, Dr. Angelou became one of her dear friends. That experience changed her completely. She got her life back on track, concentrated on her education, and returned to public speaking, a talent that later took her to places. In 1970, she won a speaking competition at the local Elks' Club in which the prize was a four-year college scholarship.

In 1971, she was selected to attend the White House Conference on Youth in Colorado. She represented Tennessee alongside other students. When she returned back, Nashville's WVOL radio station requested an interview with the enthusiastic teenager. This brought about another opportunity when the station asked her to represent them in the Miss Fire Prevention beauty pageant. She became the first African-American to win the competition. Oprah's first experience in journalism came from the same radio station. She accepted an offer to hear her voice on tape after the beauty pageant. She was no stranger to public speaking, so it was only natural to accept, which led to a part-time position reading the news.

When she turned 17, she finished out her senior year of high school and remained working at the station. She had already secured a full college scholarship, and her future was bright. She attended Tennessee State University and was crowned Miss Black Tennessee at 18, and went on to build a successful career in media. Today, Oprah Winfrey is a popular name both locally and internationally.

Therefore, I encourage everyone going through any difficulty to be strong and courageous. Do not be weary; God will make all things beautiful in His time."

NOTES

1. Agada: A locally made collapsible wooden chair.
2. Amaokwu: A hypothetical Igbo village. It is a name mostly given to a village perceived as being troublesome.
3. Amauwani: A hypothetical Igbo village. It is a name mostly given to a village at the outskirt of a town.
4. Adanma: A beautiful damsel.
5. Akara: Bean cake.
6. Amaokpala: A place or community named after the first son.
7. Atikpa: A stubborn fellow.
8. Chi: God.
9. Chim oo: An exclamation meaning "Oh my God."
10. Chiemerie: God is victorious.

11. Chizoba: God's continual protection.

12. Chioma: Good God.

13. Chukwudi: God exists.

14. Dike: Strong and mighty: A name given to a person perceived to be strong.

15. Dikeukwu: A strong and mighty man of valor.

16. Eke market: A well-known market; one of the four market days in Igbo land.

17. Jonny just come: A common parlance used in describing a person who has just relocated to an environment or who isn't familiar with an environment.

18. Egusi soup: An Igbo soup made from melon seeds.

19. Ichie: A titled man or a chief.

20. Igbo: An ethnic group in South Eastern part of Nigeria.

21. Liz: Short form of the name Elizabeth.

22. Miri: Water.

23. Mama: Mother.

24. Munachi: God is with me.

25. Mama Uka: Uka's mother.

26. Manjara: A local lantern powered by either kerosene or paraffin.

27. Mr. Ojo: A male name peculiar to the Yoruba tribe of Nigeria.

28. Nneka: Mother is great or mother is the precious; a popular name given to a girl child.

29. Nzu: Calabash chalk used either for writing on a black board or for pouring libations to the gods or ancestors.

30. Obiageli: A female Igbo name meaning "Whoever comes shall eat."

31. Osinachi: It comes from God.

32. Odukwu: A shrine highly dreaded in Igbo land because it is believed to kill its convicted victims through thunder and lightning.

33. Osukwu: A succulent palm fruit.

34. Obi: A special hut for the man of the house; usually erected in front of the main house for receiving visitors.

35. Okpa: A delicious Igbo snack made from Bambara nut seed.

36. Onitsha: The biggest city in South Eastern Nigeria.

37. Okwuoto Ekene-eze: Refers to a truck or SUV (Utility Vehicle).

38. Oyibo Magic: Foreign or exotic magic.

39. Onuku: A stupid or a dull person.

40. Oya: Let's start or let's begin something; or a speech signaling someone to start an act.

41. Osiso: Be quick or take swift action.

42. Omugwo: An Igbo postpartum tradition among the Igbo people where a mother provides support for a given time to her daughter who just gave birth.

43. Osuofia: An Igbo name meaning a pace-setter.

44. Roban: Shopping malls located at various cities in South Eastern Nigeria.

45. Tina: A short form of the name Clementina.

46. Ukwa: African bread fruit.

47. Uloaku: An Igbo name signifying house of wealth or riches or a bank.

48. Ukadike: This refers to discussions that are considered deep; not superficial.

49. Ugomma: An embodiment of beauty.

50. Uche: Means "Intention, will, mind or sense.

51. Upper Iweka: A terminal for travelers who come to Onitsha from different parts of the country.

52. Utali: A cane or whip.

53. Uwadiegwu: The world is full of fears, surprises, and mysteries.

54. Uchenna: A name of African origin meaning God's mind or God's wish.

55. Udoka: Peace is the ultimate or peace is great.

56. Ugba: A Nigerian cuisine made from sliced African oil bean seed.

Made in the USA
Columbia, SC
10 November 2021

48507955R00150